DOUBLE FOR DEATH

Double For Death

A Patrick Dawlish Mystery

**John Creasey *writing as*
Gordon Ashe**

ISBN: 978-1-5040-9873-1

This edition published in 2025 by Open Road Integrated Media, Inc.
180 Maiden Lane
New York, NY 10038
www.openroadmedia.com

DOUBLE FOR DEATH

CHAPTER I

COOL RECEPTION

Patrick Dawlish walked up the stairs to his flat, whistling. At the landing windows, the evening sun shone and the blue sky comforted the eye, and all looked well. With Dawlish, all was well. Life was good, business was good, and his wife was waiting for him, not only good but lovely. So the tune that Dawlish whistled was gay and lilting, and at each landing his pace quickened, until he was performing what was remarkably like a two-step.

At his front door, a bright green front door on the top landing, he stopped. Here, the sun shone from behind him, throwing his shadow upon the door, making the brightly polished brass of letterbox and bellpush glint and gleam. He took out his key, and found the keyhole at the first attempt, evidence that he was completely sober. In fact, only high spirits explained the whistling and the gleam in his eyes and the sense of expectancy.

He opened the door.

His wife, in a dress of wine red, came from his study.

Now it is understood the world over that a man can judge his wife's mood in a flash of time. The moods of other women might deceive him, but never his wife's. Her smile might be as sweet as honey from the bee, but if her mood is sour, then he will sense it before a word is spoken.

He did not think that Felicity's mood was simply sour. He was sure that she was not in the receptive mood that his high spirits needed. Something was not quite right; that showed in her eyes and the smile of her full lips even when she greeted:

"Hallo, darling."

"Hallo, my sweet, it's good to see you." When uncertain, Dawlish, as all men, played safe and was not extravagant. The kiss he gave her was emphatic, but on the cheeks. "Sorry I'm later than I hoped, but it isn't seven yet, is it?"

"No," said Felicity.

Dawlish knew, then, that whatever was on her mind was *not* his lateness. He had not forgotten some special reason for reaching home at a given time, so his conscience could stay clear. He slid an arm round her slim waist and they turned towards the study, the door of which stood open. This was a pleasant room, furnished with antiques of various periods, with a brown carpet which muffled footsteps, and a window which overlooked a green, open space. This was evening, and London had a quiet air.

"Odd little man showed up just before we were closing," Dawlish said, "and I had to look after him myself. An Egyptian who looked as if he'd walked straight out of one of the Pyramids."

"Really," said Felicity, and eyed him up and down.

There was a pause.

"Darling," said Dawlish, "what have I done wrong?"

"Oh, nothing at all," said Felicity airily. "How could the lord and master do anything wrong?"

At that moment, Dawlish knew that whatever he had done, it had affected her very deeply. It must be a grievous kind of oversight. He searched his mind, almost desperately. Wedding anniversary? No. Birthday? No. His mind was blank and his conscience crystal clear, yet he was uneasy.

"Not guilty," he said, in a praiseworthy attempt to sound nonchalant. "What is it?"

"But *Patrick*, of course you're not guilty," said Felicity. She had a pleasing voice, rather low-pitched, and although not classically beautiful, she was most certainly lovely to him. Nice. Wholesome. Her eyes were grey-green with golden flecks and full of vitality, her lips were full but nicely shaped, and her fair complexion was without a blemish. Her hair was a little more fair than dark, and a few strands of grey were lost in natural waves drawn back from her forehead with a centre parting. "After all, things have changed since we moved from Haslemere, haven't they? I have my work and you have yours and why should they ever meet?" she said.

It was almost a gibe.

Dawlish took out his cigarettes and lit one with great deliberation.

"Why, indeed?" he remarked, for the sake of saying something.

"I have to be the perfect receptionist, and be nice to all Lydia's customers. Most of them are about to step into the grave, but occasionally I get a handsome young man." Felicity paused, as if to deliver a mortal thrust. "In fact the day before yesterday one of them made a pass at me."

"His name?" asked Dawlish, firmly.

"Oh, but why should you worry about *me*? I can look after myself, can't I? After all, the cameraman is about most of the time. And in any case, can't we *trust* each other?" Felicity paused again, but only to gather strength, and her eyes were sparkling.

Dawlish recognized the mood now, as one of danger, but he could not understand it, although he was beginning to comprehend the basic cause. Jealousy was jealousy, whether there was a good, justifiable reason for it or not.

"You have adopted the shop and your funny old men who were related to the Pharaohs," Felicity declared with wounding sarcasm. "Isn't it strange how I always hear about the old and the odd and the hag-like customers, *never* the sweet young things?"

In jealousy, there is no logic.

It was pointless to remind her that this was not true and that in calmer moods she would laugh at herself for suggesting it. Dawlish tried hard to think why she was behaving like it. At certain times he would have understood in a moment, for he had a reputation as a detective, and another for taking risks. She disliked both. Had he been busy on some investigation without having told her, her mood might have been easily explained. But in that way life had been uneventful of late.

In another way, it had been full of excitement. For friends in London, Lydia and Maurice Gale, had gone abroad for a long, long trip, and the Dawlishes had become partners in the businesses that the Gales ran, and now were in full charge. Dawlish was in charge at *Gale's,* a curio and antique business in the West End; Felicity of the photographic studio, next door to this flat in St. John's Wood. Each had experts to assist them; until today both—as far as Dawlish knew—were having fun.

Felicity behaving like this was not even remotely funny.

"Is that all you can do—stand there and look foolish?" Felicity cried, becoming almost waspish.

Dawlish laughed. He couldn't help it, because the flash of anger lit up her face and put fire into her eyes, making her very lovely to look at but comic in an intimate, precious way. As the laugh came, however, he knew that it was grievously timed indeed. He tried to put an arm round her shoulders but she slid away from him, and her eyes still stormed. He stopped laughing, but continued to smile; yet he had never seen her looking angrier, and his disquiet was very great indeed.

"So it's *funny*," she breathed. "You can laugh in my face, after—after—" she caught her breath, swung away from him, and stared towards the window. He saw her shoulders move; she was crying. This had become really serious; to her it was tremendously important; and he could understand nothing except that he had to help her.

He had the sense to stand and wait. She did not cry easily or often; in fact, in a few minutes she would be capable of denying that she had cried at all. But she averted her eyes, even when she raised her head and had obviously won command over herself.

Dawlish spoke in a quiet, practical voice.

"All right, now tell me what I've done, and I'll try to see why it's upset you."

She turned to face him; and there were tears in her eyes. Her mood had changed completely, which was a relief; yet he could see that she was really deeply affected, that she was afraid that there was something drastically wrong between them.

"Pat, don't pretend," she said. "I know that this kind of thing does happen, but at least we can be honest about it."

He put his head on one side.

"Honesty above all," he agreed solemnly. "I swear to tell you the truth, the whole truth, and nothing but the truth."

"Pat, *please*—"

"Darling, there isn't a feather on my conscience," Dawlish said, and took her arm. "Let's have a drink." He led her towards the cocktail cabinet, which was in fact an old Jacobean court cupboard, magnificently carved and polished over the centuries until it was almost black. "I haven't done a thing you'd disapprove of. I haven't been to Scotland Yard for months. I haven't shown any interest in crime. No beauteous young maiden has come pleading for my help. Business has been business—buying and selling *objets d'art* and curios to Maurice Gale's pals—wealthy Egyptians, Persians, South Americans, Japanese—"

"Pat!"

"It's true," he said.

She stared as if she were beginning to doubt her fears for the first time. The look on her face, in the moment when doubt was born, almost made him laugh again; he checked himself, and poured out a sherry for her, a whisky-and-soda for himself.

"Let's drink to it," he said. "My virgin conscience, I mean."

He sipped.

"Pat, I can't—oh, no, this is ridiculous," said Felicity, and seemed to shake herself. "She came here this afternoon. I saw her in here. I talked to her, and she is—"

She stopped.

Dawlish sipped again.

"Darling," he said, "this really is beginning to intrigue me. Who is she and what is she? Would you rather have gin? Or a whisky—"

"No—no, thanks." Felicity drank a little sherry. "Give me a cigarette," she said, and held his fingers while he lit it for her, leaned against him for a moment; he could sense the relief which went through her whole body, her heart and mind. "But I don't understand."

"That," said Dawlish firmly, "is mutual."

"But she *knows* it's you."

"Well, that wouldn't be a crime even if I knew her too, would it?" asked Dawlish. "Young, comely—"

"She met you in Madrid."

Dawlish, his mouth open to taste the whisky again, stopped with his lips an inch or two from the glass, and stared. He did not look at his best at that moment, although he was, as always, remarkably handsome but for his broken nose. He was tall and massive and his fair hair had natural waves, now flecked with grey, he had good eyes, blue as the sky, good features but for that battered nose, and something more than that, an air—in the days of old it would have been called swashbuckling—a kind of grandeur.

"Oh, no," he said weakly. "No."

"You *do* know her." Accusation put an edge to Felicity's voice.

"Well, it's possible." He was expansive, reasoning. "I met several señoritas who weren't exactly sweet young things and who weren't accompanied by their duennas, but—"

"You next saw her in Milan, in October."

"I did not see any Spanish señorita in Milan in October," asseverated Dawlish.

"And in Zurich, in January."

"Oh, no, I didn't," declared Dawlish. "In fact I don't recall having anything to do with any unattached young women, whether from Spain, Italy, Switzerland or—"

"You were with her in Paris in April!"

"This," said Dawlish, "has gone too far." He finished his drink; for the first time he felt that he really needed one. He poured himself another, and tried to keep the conversation on a matter-of-fact level, but his thoughts were chaotic. He had made several trips abroad, on Maurice Gale's behalf; and had visited all the places Felicity had named, but. . . . "Now let me see. A Spanish girl of no mean charm—"

"She's quite beautiful," Felicity said slowly, reluctantly. "She really is. Her eyes—"

"Yes, they have nice eyes," Dawlish agreed solemnly. "So a beautiful Spanish girl with magnificent eyes has told you that we met in Madrid—"

"Met," said Felicity, "is a euphemism. There was a certain degree of intimacy in this association."

Dawlish was reduced to silent bewilderment.

"And also in Milan and in Zurich and in Paris," said Felicity. "In fact, you spent your honeymoon in Paris."

That was the really bad moment.

Dawlish had poured out his second drink, and was contemplating it as well as Felicity's eyes. Now, he gulped it down, and turned, found a chair just behind him, and dropped into it. Felicity stared, as if wondering whether his reaction betrayed some form of guilt; but although he was shaken, he was sure that she had worked the doubt out of her system.

"Listen," he said at last. "This is slander. No, it's worse. It's attempting to come between man and wife. An accusation of bigamy from a Spanish—" he gulped. "No," he said, and squared his shoulders. "*No*," he boomed. "May you be forgiven, you Delilah, you've been leading me up the garden, and—"

He jumped to his feet, suddenly gay, light-hearted, ready to laugh at himself for taking her seriously.

"I haven't!" Felicity cried. "I'm—it's true."

"It can't be! The whole thing is crazy, preposterous, ludicrous, nonsensical! Listen, my love, it's a hoax and you fell for it. I can hardly believe that you'd swallow it hook, line and sinker, but—"

"It is not a practical joke," Felicity said, shrilly. There was a strange look in her eyes now, a look that was alarmed, bewildered, agitated. "*I* knew you hadn't married her, but she believes you have."

He raised his arms heavenwards.

"But my darling, none of this makes sense. How could anyone believe that I married her and spent a honeymoon in Paris? It's—" he broke off, closed his eyes for a moment, and then felt overwhelmed by the desire to giggle. It *must* be a hoax; what else? He gave a kind of exhausted laugh, and went back to his chair. "Of course it doesn't make sense. And you know it. You're rehearsing some damned play, or—"

"Pat, I am not! She was here. She thought I was *Miss* Dawlish, your sister. I didn't disabuse her. I—I wanted to learn all I could. She gave *her* name as Mrs. Mepita Dawlish. She is *beautiful*. And—she's coming back."

Dawlish did not speak.

Felicity eyed him with fresh tension.

It seemed a long time before anything happened, and when it did, it was outside the room. It was a short, sharp ring at the front door. The sound went through Dawlish like an electric shock.

Their maid, also inherited, walked heavily across the hall to open the door.

"I wish we'd never come here," Felicity sniffed.

He did not take advantage of that momentary weakness. For it had been Felicity who had urged them to leave their home in Surrey, the orchards and the piggeries which Dawlish doted on, for London. They had let their home and everything with it for three years, the first of which was nearly over.

Now she wished she'd never come.

CHAPTER II

A YOUNG MAN FROM SPAIN

The maid said, "Good evening."

There was a pause, and during it Dawlish rose slowly to his feet and stepped towards the door, which was ajar; he hoped to see the caller before the caller saw him.

A man said: "Good evening. Is Mr. Patrick Dawlish here, please?"

The fact that the caller was male brought some relief; but that was offset by his voice. He was not English. His words were precise enough and there could be no mistaking them, but the accent was unmistakably that of a foreigner. It wasn't French and it wasn't northern European; Spanish or Italian Dawlish judged, sure that he wasn't far wrong.

"I'll find out," the maid said. "Will you wait a minute, please?"

"Of course," said the man, who sounded young.

There was a pause, then the door closed and a moment later Alice's heavy footsteps sounded as she came towards the study. Alice had been with the Gales for many years, had left to get married, had married and returned—obviously unhappy but not prepared to talk of her disappointments. She had a room next door, but preferred her kitchen and was in the flat at all hours, whether officially on duty or not.

She tapped at the door.

"Come in," Felicity called, apparently bewildered.

"It's a gentleman to see Mr. Dawlish," announced Alice, on whom training in the niceties of decorum had been completely wasted. She held out a card. "I haven't told him that Mr. Dawlish's in," she added, in a voice so loud that the caller could not possibly fail to hear.

Dawlish took the card, and read without any particular surprise:

CARLOS DE CIENTO Y FERNANDEZ
Avenida Republica, 698, Barcelona

Felicity read this over Dawlish's shoulder.

"*Are* you in?" asked Alice.

She was a buxom young woman with lank, mousy hair, locks of which hung on her forehead. Her cheeks were flushed, because she was putting the finishing touches to dinner; and her manner suggested that Felicity ought to have beaten her to the front door and she couldn't be blamed if the potatoes were scorched. The sleeves of her blue smock were rolled up to the elbows.

"Yes. I'll bring Mr. Fernandez in," Felicity said, and forced a smile which must have cost a great effort. "You'll have to see him, Pat, won't you?"

"Yes, ma'am," Dawlish said meekly.

Alice went out; and Felicity followed.

Felicity had obviously made up her mind to get the first look at the young man with the Spanish name and the accent; and Dawlish did not greatly mind about that. He had a minute, at most, in which to think; and made no use of that time at all. He could recall no one whom he had met in Madrid, Milan, Zurich or Paris who might cause him a moment's anxiety—unless someone wanted to rake up the really distant past.

"Do go in," Felicity said, in her sweetest voice, and ushered a young man in. "Darling, this is Señor Fernandez," she went on.

She smiled, too.

The young man was tall, beautifully proportioned, and so handsome that he did not seem to be real. He was dressed in a suit of biscuit-coloured cloth; and the suit fitted him perfectly. He stepped, as it were, straight out of a slick magazine or Hollywood; and by far the most impressive feature was his eyes. The rest was so impressive that this made his eyes utterly astonishing. They were dark brown, velvety, almost black; and so large, so luminous, that they seemed to spread a light.

His features, beautifully regular, hardly seemed to matter. His jet black hair might have been set by an expert.

He stopped in front of Dawlish. His eyes glowed, he inclined his head a little, and he smiled. He had excellent teeth, and his lips were not only well shaped but very red.

"Mr. Dawlish," he said, "I am very happy indeed to meet you. *Very* happy." He took Dawlish's hand as if he meant to hold on to it for a long time, and would not let go. He shook it vigorously. "I am very, *very* happy to meet you," he repeated, and his eyes seemed to travel from the top of Dawlish's head to the tip of his toes and back again; as if he were looking for some flaw, some fault which did not show immediately.

It was true that, man for man, Dawlish did not compare unfavourably—the Saxon contrasting with the Southern European to make a picture worth seeing.

"How are you?" Dawlish murmured.

"I cannot say *how* happy I am to meet you," said Carlos de

Ciento y Fernandez, and still squeezed Dawlish's hand. "My sister has told me so much about you."

Felicity echoed "Sister," faintly. Dawlish, falling back on inanity, said, "Oh, really," and took out his cigarettes. "Will you smoke?" He disengaged his hand, and pressed first cigarettes and then sherry upon Fernandez, who had now started to look about the room as if assessing its value in much the same way as he had assessed Dawlish's person. Obviously he was satisfied, because his smile was almost smug.

"She will soon be here," he announced, and sat down.

Dawlish said: "Who will soon be here?"

This question obviously amused Fernandez, who said: "Mepita, my sister, Mr. Dawlish. She could not come with me, she had to see a friend, but she will not be long."

He stretched out his legs, as if ready for a long stay. The winged armchair was two hundred years old, and they were not made more comfortable even in these days of foam rubber and pneumatic cushioning. Somehow, the chair seemed right for him. He had an air of belonging to a gallant, bygone age.

It would have been comparatively easy to cope at that stage had Dawlish known nothing of Felicity's story. With that vivid in his mind he hardly knew how to begin. Obviously, this was his 'bigamous wife's' brother. Obviously, Fernandez expected to be welcomed as a brother-in-law. As obviously, he was going to get a severe shock; the difficulty was deciding just how to administer it. Looking into the handsome face, Dawlish saw or imagined qualities of fiery temper and of great pride. Fernandez would not take kindly to being told that there had been an error. It was at least probable that he would refuse to believe it.

Dawlish tried to gain a little time while probing gently.

"How long have you been in London?"

"Just for some hours, like my sister," said Fernandez. "We

flew from Madrid, and arrived at London Airport early this morning." He smiled amiably at Felicity. Obviously he was greatly interested in Felicity, which gave Dawlish some breathing space. "Do you like flying?"

There was something new in his manner now, perhaps a hint that he was puzzled because he had not yet been introduced. It would be wise to let him remain puzzled, but how *had* this mistake come about? It was ludicrous—it was everything Dawlish had said to Felicity, yet it carried much disquiet. Fernandez and the girl had the right name and the right address, so it was not a simple matter of mistaken identity.

"Not very much." Felicity was groping desperately, too. It should be funny, ludicrously funny; but it wasn't.

Dawlish decided to put an end to the fencing.

To fortify himself, he mixed himself another drink and did not drown the whisky.

"Señor Fernandez." He was brisk.

"Yes, Mr. Dawlish?" Fernandez beamed.

"Why have you and your sister come to England?"

"Why? But you know," said Fernandez, and unexpectedly gave a laugh; it wasn't very free, he did not like this question. He sat up in his chair, and Dawlish became more certain than ever that the Spaniard would be a bad man to cross. "You have sold the jewels for us, everything is now settled." Fernandez paused, and looked suspiciously at Dawlish, his expression very different from what it had been. "Is that not true?"

Dawlish said slowly, deliberately: "What jewels?"

He had expected an outburst; he had practically set out to cause one. All those uncertainties, the feeling that this was very complicated and possibly alarming, rose to the surface.

Maurice Gale did much business in precious stones, and a year ago he and Dawlish had visited Spain together, seeking a collection for a wealthy buyer. Dawlish had a passing knowledge of gems; and Gale had taught him much more. He wasn't really an expert but he was well on the way.

Gale had customers in Spain, too; some of them had visited the West End shop from time to time, and talked to Dawlish.

But Dawlish had never heard of Carlos de Ciento y Fernandez, or his sister, or their jewels.

It was as if drums were beating in the distance; the drums of suspicion, of warning, of alarm.

Fernandez stood up, slowly.

He was as tall as Dawlish, who stood more than six feet, bodily was a rapier to Dawlish's broadsword. The smile vanished from his face. The haughtiness, which had been noticeable before, turned unmistakably into arrogance. Anger darkened his cheeks.

"I do not understand you," he said stiffly.

"There's a lot we don't understand," Dawlish told him quietly. "What jewels am I supposed to have sold for you?"

Fernandez did not answer at once, but his hands clenched and he raised them aggressively. His eyes blazed, his lips curved back but did not part; stretched as they were, they gave him a dangerous look. He was not acting; this was the nature of the man.

"I do not understand you," he repeated. "You are Patrick Dawlish, the business friend of Maurice Gale. You are my sister's husband. She entrusted you with the sale of *our* jewels." The words came very softly. "That is so," he went on, and took a half step forward. "Answer me—you *are* Patrick Dawlish?"

Dawlish said: "Yes. Now take it easy. I haven't seen your sister, as far as I know. The first I heard of her was when my wife—"

Fernandez cried: "Your *wife*? *This* woman?"

Loathing, contempt, anger all echoed in his words and showed in his expression. He rounded on Felicity, and she backed a pace in sudden alarm. His eyes showed the burning heat of his anger and his temper. He was motionless for a moment, glaring at Felicity. Then he turned swiftly on Dawlish, and struck out.

Dawlish saw it coming.

Here was a man fifteen years younger than he, physically powerful, fit, and in a flaming temper. He could do a lot of damage, if he were given the chance. Physical violence had become an art form with Pat Dawlish, and he became artistic now. He struck the Spaniard sharply in the stomach, bringing his head forward, clipped him under the chin and, as he staggered back, grabbed his right wrist and twisted it. Fernandez stopped moving. His arm was locked, he was helpless—and looked bewildered and bemused.

Dawlish said mildly: "We don't have to behave like children, do we? I'm as anxious as you are to find out what this is all about. You may have been fooled and you may have been swindled, but I know nothing about it." He did not twist the other's wrist enough to hurt; but he held him there. "Are we going to talk reasonably or do we want to get hurt?"

Fernandez's lips were parted now; the rage still flamed, but a new expression crept into his eyes; bewilderment? Dawlish held on for thirty seconds, then let the man go. He turned away deliberately, saw alarm spring into Felicity's eyes, but did not think there would be any more trouble from the Spaniard—yet.

Fernandez shrugged his coat into position, and rubbed his wrist slowly. He did not look away from Dawlish, the bewilderment didn't fade. There was silence except for the chink of glass as Dawlish poured another drink for Felicity.

Then abruptly: "I am sorry about that, Mr. Dawlish," Fernandez said. "I should not have lost my temper." His voice was cold and hostile, but he had himself in complete control.

"I'm not so sure," Dawlish said amiably: "In your place I'd have acted first and thought about it afterwards. Wouldn't you, Fel?" He hoped to thaw Fernandez out, wanted the whole story told without the bias that anger would give it. "Your sister— I imagine it was your sister—was here this afternoon, and my wife saw her. It was obvious that there was some misunderstanding." He gave a smile that was nearly a laugh. "It must be some other Dawlish."

Fernandez said slowly: "Yes, perhaps that is it." He was not persuaded by a long way, suspicion still showed dark in his eyes. "Tell me, *are* you Patrick Dawlish who is a partner in Gale's business?"

"Yes."

Fernandez said chokily: "Then it is not a mistake, you are the right man!" His fists clenched. "You have done this to Mepita, you—"

"Listen, Fernandez," Dawlish interrupted briskly. "Either there's another Dawlish or someone has impersonated me, making you and your sister believe that he is the Dawlish of *Gale's*. There isn't another antique and jewel merchant trading in London under the same name, and I'm in charge there. You'll have to believe the facts."

"I am beginning to understand," Fernandez said slowly. In that moment he looked very young, and gave the impression that some horror was gradually taking possession of him. He moved back, as if to sit down, but stood by the arm of his chair. "And yet—yet Mepita believes that she is married to—to you," he said. "She trusted the jewels to you."

He stopped; but Dawlish did not prompt him.

"Why isn't she here?" Fernandez asked thinly. "What time is it?" He glanced at his wrist-watch. "It is half past *seven*. She was to meet me here *at* seven. I was a little late, I—"

He paused again.

His rage came back, turning his cheeks a dusky red, glittering in his eyes, making him clench his hands. If he had no other troubles, controlling his temper would always give him plenty to think about.

"She has been here," he said viciously. "Where is she? What have you done with Mepita? You have lied to me, lied to her; you are the man to whom she gave the jewels, whom she trusted, whom she married. *Where is my sister?*"

CHAPTER III

TALK OF A LOST LADY

Dawlish moved away from the young Spaniard and lit a cigarette, trying to behave in a way which would ease the tension. Felicity had hardly moved for the last ten minutes; now she glanced at Dawlish swiftly, understanding his problem.

"I demand the answer," Fernandez said. "Where is Mepita?"

"I wish I knew," said Dawlish warmly. "I hope she'll soon be here. She will be able to convince you that whoever did take the jewels, it wasn't I." He drew deeply on the cigarette, realizing that Fernandez was so full of suspicion that he could hardly think clearly. "If she doesn't come soon," he went on, "we ought to go to the police."

"The *police*?" Fernandez echoed.

That brought another change of expression, and with it came an unmistakable touch of fear. Dawlish had thought that everything that could happen on one evening had already happened; he discovered that he was wrong. By suggesting the police he had hoped to reassure Fernandez; instead, he had scared him. A frightened man was more likely to lose his temper again.

"Listen, Fernandez—" he began.

"I do not want to listen to you," Fernandez interrupted brusquely. "I can now understand what has happened. Mepita came here this afternoon, and discovered that you were already married. She accused you of this villainy, and you—"

"Kidnapped her," suggested Dawlish, mildly. Laughter gleamed in his bright blue eyes—an attempt to break through the young man's tension by showing that he was not worried at all; but he wasn't sure that he would succeed. "No, nothing like that happened. We'll probably find it's all a mistake, and when she comes she'll realize it at once. I'm sorry if—"

"Sorry!" exclaimed the Spaniard. "*Sorry!*" He raised clenched hands and shook them at the ceiling. "Am I talking to a block of wood? Mepita *married* a man whom she believed to be you. She entrusted him with all our possessions, with a fortune!" He stopped again, and obviously all his suspicions poured back; and who could blame him? "I do not believe you," he said deliberately. "I believe that you are the man, that you betrayed her to get the jewels, that you have kept her away from me. *Where is Mepita?*"

Dawlish said: 'That's all nonsense. She'll be here in a few minutes. Have another drink, sit down, and wait."

Fernandez didn't speak.

Felicity said: "I must go and have a word with Alice," and went out.

Dawlish waited with the Spaniard, ears strained to catch the sound of a caller; but no one came.

It was Felicity who suggested that Fernandez should dine with them, while waiting. He accepted the invitation with stiff courtesy.

"A little trifle and ice cream?" Felicity asked, half an hour later.

"Thank you, no," said Fernandez stiffly.

"Some fruit?"

"Thank you, no."

"Coffee?"

"If you please."

Felicity turned to the table by her side, where Alice had put the coffee, which was on a hote-plate. Fernandez glanced at her, then looked back at Dawlish. He had watched Dawlish second by second since he had talked of his loss of jewels, seemed to be afraid that if he took his gaze away Dawlish would vanish into thin air.

The tension, great at first, had become unbearable.

He had picked at his meal; yet Alice had done full justice to English food. Dawlish had felt that it was almost a sin to have an appetite, but Felicity hadn't done too badly.

"Will you have a brandy?" Dawlish suggested, and moved his chair back. The dining-room was small, and the brandy was in a William and Mary corner cupboard.

"No!" Fernandez almost barked.

Dawlish said: "I hope you'll change your mind," and stood up and went to the cupboard. "You, darling?"

"No, thanks."

Dawlish brought Courvoisier and Drambuie from the cupboard. Fernandez stared at him with burning eyes. Felicity pushed her plate away, finished serving the coffee, and handed Fernandez his cup.

"Thank you." He could hardly get the words out.

"It's nearly nine," Dawlish said, "and I think we should make inquiries. I also think we should call in the police."

Seconds passed before Fernandez spoke; he seemed to fight for words. At last he said with great deliberation:

"You know that I cannot call in the police, but—I have *friends*. I shall avenge myself, and avenge Mepita. Do not make the mistake of thinking that you will succeed. I shall find Mepita, and after that . . ."

Dawlish poured Courvoisier into a tiny glass.

"I can't stop you from talking like a fool, but I'm getting tired of it," he said brusquely. "Call the Spanish Embassy, call anyone you like in London, and you'll get proof of my good standing. I've never met your sister. It looks as if I've been impersonated, and that whoever convinced Mepita that he was Dawlish of *Gale's* now knows that the game's up. He may have found a way to stop her from coming here. We must try to find out, and the best way is to tell the police."

Fernandez said through his teeth: "You know that I cannot go to the police."

"Why not?"

"You *know*!"

"Oh, to merry blazes with this!" Dawlish said in exasperation, and jumped up again. "I'm going to call Scotland Yard, and we'll let them sort it out." He moved towards the door as Fernandez moved, evaded the man's outstretched hand and strode into the study. He was at the telephone when the Spaniard rushed in; Felicity wasn't far behind him.

"You shall not tell the police!"

"Don't you want to find your sister?"

"You know where she is!"

"I don't know a thing about her." Dawlish held the telephone but did not dial. "Why are you scared of the police? What is this—a blackmail racket?"

"You know—"

"I don't know a thing except that you seem to be crazy," Dawlish said, and dialled WHI 1212. There was the sound of the dialling; and of the Spaniard's heavy breathing. "Hallo. . . . Is Superintendent Trivett there, please? . . . Yes, I'll hold on."

He looked up into Fernandez's face.

Fernandez tried to snatch the receiver from his hand. Dawlish kept it free, made ready for another attack—and then there was a sharp ring at the front door-bell. The thing they had been waiting for had come in the very moment when they had forgotten it. The ring made Fernandez swing round, made Dawlish jump, made Felicity run towards the door with the Spaniard after her.

At the Yard, the operator said: "No, he's at home. Shall I put you through to—"

"No, thanks, forget it." Dawlish banged the telephone down, and hurried to the door. He was in time to see Felicity open it; Fernandez with a hand at her shoulder; and a youth who was almost hidden by them.

"Name o' Dawlish?" the youth demanded, pertly.

"Yes," Felicity said, breathlessly.

"Special delivery," the youth said, and handed her a letter. "Ta."

He turned away and hurried, whistling, towards the head of the stairs. Fernandez seemed struck dumb with disappointment. Felicity stared at the letter. Dawlish tore the letter open, glanced at it, then thrust it back into Felicity's hand and pushed past both of them. He watched the youth, who was in his late teens, hurrying down the first flight of stairs.

Dawlish went after him.

He heard Fernandez exclaim, turned back, and hurried into the hall.

"Dawlish—" began the Spaniard.

"Pat!" gasped Felicity.

"Try to knock some sense into his head," Dawlish growled. "It's too late for special delivery; I want to trace that messenger." He slammed the door, waited for a moment, then switched off the light. "I'm going to follow the boy, Fernandez. You stay here."

"If you leave, I—"

Dawlish said: "If you try to stop me, the police will be here within ten minutes. I'll make quite sure of that."

Fernandez didn't move or speak.

Dawlish opened the door, and stepped on to the landing. Felicity, knowing what he was doing, closed the door behind him. He kept close to the wall, and went down the stairs; half-way down, he heard the street door close. Soon it would be locked, but it was always left open until ten o'clock.

Dawlish reached the hall, and opened the street door in time to see the youth climbing on to a motor-cycle.

His own car was parked a few yards along.

The youth didn't glance at the door, but started off, the two-stroke engine popping merrily. He headed for Regent's Park. Dawlish reached his car, a big Humber, and was at the wheel and moving off when the youth turned left at the end of the road, Withy Street, towards the West End. Dawlish sent his car hurtling towards the corner, was ready to swing left when a man stepped into the road.

One moment the road was empty; next, the man was there, walking as if blindly towards the Humber. Dawlish jammed on his brakes. The tyres squealed. The man looked up with a start. His face showed clearly in a street lamp—a pale face with thick-lensed glasses and thick lips, a startled expression, a snub nose.

Two cars and a lorry passed the end of the street.

The man scurried back to the pavement he had started from, looking scared and apologetic.

Dawlish turned into the main road, but it was already too late. He couldn't see the red light of the motor-cycle, which might have taken any turning to the left or might be hidden by the other traffic on the road. It would be a waste of time going any further. He glowered at the back of the man with the thick-lensed glasses, who was now walking on the pavement thirty yards away, then turned the car and drove to his house.

He went in.

He did not go upstairs immediately, but waited, then opened the street door and watched the street. He saw no one; no shadows; nothing to suggest that anyone was there. He felt uneasy, full of foreboding. The timing of the letter, the behaviour of the Spaniard, the failure of the girl to appear, all made their contribution.

He imagined danger where there might be none.

Felicity's nerves wouldn't take too much of this kind of thing. Fernandez was either a most accomplished actor or a young man sitting on top of a volcano.

Dawlish turned towards the stairs.

If Fernandez were telling the truth what must he feel like? His sister had gone through a form of marriage; a fortune in jewels had vanished. . . .

Dawlish began to dislike the set-up very much indeed. It was more comforting to doubt whether the jewels existed, to assume that Fernandez and his sister were working together to discredit him. But if blackmail were in their minds, would they go this way about it? They would threaten to tell Felicity, not tell her at once.

He tried to picture the girl who had come here, apparently cheerfully, eagerly, to see her 'husband'—and to imagine what she would feel like if she discovered that she had been fooled.

He reached the top landing. Light showed at the sides and bottom of the door, but it was closed. He opened it, and heard Felicity speaking; she was in the kitchen with Alice, and came out as the front door closed.

"I hoped he'd tell us where the letter came from, but he got away," Dawlish said sadly. "Seen the letter?"

Felicity said, "Yes. Fernandez took it," and her tone as well as her expression told him that it was not good. "Darling, be very careful with him."

"The letter wasn't really meant for Fernandez," Dawlish murmured, half to himself. "Someone decided to tell him to go back to Spain and forget all about the jewels, if he ever wants to see Mepita again."

"Yes," Felicity said. "And he's sure that it's a trick, that you're behind it all, and he could be dangerous. His temper's as bad—"

"I know," said Dawlish. He squeezed her arm, then moved towards the study, the door of which was open. He could see Fernandez's shadow against the wall by the fireplace; the Spaniard was standing still—very still.

Dawlish said carelessly: "There must be a way of making him understand that I know nothing about it." He stepped softly to the door as he spoke, and peered through the crack at the side. He could just see Fernandez, but couldn't make out everything he wanted to. He spoke again, more quietly, as if he were further from the door. "If he won't believe it, we can take it for granted that he's working some new racket on us."

He could see just what he wanted, now.

Fernandez was standing with his right arm raised, and a small gun in it, pointing towards the door.

CHAPTER IV

BARGAIN

Dawlish moved back from the door, and glanced at Felicity with a finger at his lips; sufficient to warn her. He spoke again, in a muted voice:

"I'll try to make him see reason."

Dawlish could go in and take a chance that Fernandez was only trying to frighten him; but with a temper like his, anything could happen, and Dawlish was never in favour of taking chances for the sake of it.

He stretched forward, took the handle of the door, and pulled it towards him. The door slammed. He heard the Spaniard shout and then jump across the room; but the key of the study door was on the outside. Dawlish turned this swiftly as Fernandez reached the door, and tugged wildly at it. The door shook violently, even the walls shook.

Alice appeared, startled, in the kitchen doorway.

Dawlish grinned at her.

"Nothing to worry about," he said soothingly, "just another man who's annoyed with me. You oughtn't to be here, anyhow."

"I—I've nearly finished," said Alice, and vanished.

Felicity said helplessly: "We can't let this go on."

"He'll cool down," Dawlish said confidently, "and when Alice's gone we can let him feel the rough edge of our tongue." He sounded much more relaxed than he felt. "It looks as if we've a new kind of problem, sweetheart. He didn't tell you why he's jittery about the police, did he?"

"Don't be an ass, of course he didn't." Felicity looked at the door, as if wishing she could see through it. Fernandez had banged once or twice, but that was all; now, he was very quiet. "I hope he doesn't start shooting."

Dawlish grinned. "Then he'd discover that we have a way with careless gunmen."

"He might discover that my jewels are in that room," Felicity said tartly.

Dawlish actually laughed.

"I'll believe a lot of things, but I won't believe that Fernandez put on this act so as to make sure that we locked him in the study so that he can crack the safe. Anyhow, he couldn't open that safe if he tried for a month."

"Couldn't he?"

"No. Stop worrying, and—"

"Darling, there *might* be others as brilliant as you are at opening safes," said Felicity with magnificent sarcasm. "I wouldn't trust you in a locked room like that for long, I'd expect to find the safe open and—"

"Forget it."

"I think we ought to send for the police now," Felicity declared, changing the subject abruptly. "We'll have to, eventually, and if we do it right away we might save ourselves a lot of trouble. He might turn violent again." When Dawlish didn't answer, she went on coldly: "I know that you're beginning to see this as a new triumph for Mr. Patrick Dawlish, the famous amateur detective, but I'm not. I don't like any of it. It's a trick to involve you—unless you really did have an *affaire* with this woman in Madrid, Milan and Zurich, with a honeymoon in Paris."

Felicity did not actually sniff.

Fernandez was very quiet.

Dawlish grinned.

"It's not funny," Felicity flared up. "Fernandez may be frightened of the police, but that's no reason why you should study his feelings. This is not a case you ought to investigate, and you know it."

"That's right," said Dawlish, mildly.

"Pat!"

"I was agreeing with you," Dawlish protested. "I wasn't very serious, it's true. Here we have a story of someone who not only impersonates me but marries a pretty girl in my name, and lifts her jewels—if the story's true—and what am I to do? Nothing?"

"Tell the police!"

"Even Bill Trivett would expect me to want to find out what's behind all this," Dawlish argued. "And he'll probably have to be told, but this certainly isn't the moment."

"Oh," said Felicity, dangerously. "And why not?"

"Because we have just one thing on Carlos de Ciento y Fernandez, and that is his fear of the police," Dawlish explained patiently. "Threatening to send for them is the most likely thing to make him put his gun away, as soon as he's had time to cool down. You wouldn't have us throw away our best chance of stopping gunplay, would you?"

"I've told you before, this is not funny!"

"You know," Dawlish said warmly, "you ought to have a holiday more often. You're too tense." He slid his arm round her waist, and squeezed. "Let's face it—what could I have done to stop this? I've never heard of Fernandez or his sister until tonight, you were actually on the scene of this job first. And if a man's impersonating me with one girl, he might be trying it with others." He put his head on one side. "We just can't stand on the sidelines for this job, can we?"

They were quiet for a long time.

No sound came from the study.

Gradually Felicity's expression relaxed. She began to smile. Her eyes glowed, reflecting the humour in Dawlish's. Complete understanding had returned between them, there was no fear now of things going awry.

Because it was good, Dawlish hugged her and chuckled.

"Darling," she said, "I knew it was crazy, but she was so certain that I did begin to wonder if you'd been having an *affaire*. I knew marriage was impossible, but she might have been putting a bold face on it. And you were in—" he kissed her—"Madrid, Milan, Zurich and Paris," she said, "alone, my sweet, alone."

He kissed her again.

Next moment something crashed down inside the study.

Dawlish felt Felicity's body stiffen as he jerked his head up. The sound echoed, something heavy had fallen to the floor. Felicity moved away from Dawlish, and Alice appeared at the kitchen door.

"W-w-w-what was *th-th-th-that*?"

Other sounds were coming from the study, now.

Dawlish turned the key, then the handle, and pushed; the door did not open, would not budge an inch. He put his shoulder to it, but it wouldn't yield; Fernandez had blocked it. Dawlish moved away, swiftly, pushing past Felicity and Alice, and rushing to the kitchen window. He flung this up, and leaned out.

Fernandez was climbing out of the window of the study,

which was in the same wall as this. He clung to a drainpipe and had a foot on the ledge of a window below. The light from the room shone on to his handsome face, half blinding him; but he looked towards Dawlish, and it was obvious that he knew Dawlish was there.

"Get back," Dawlish called sharply. "If you fall you'll break your neck."

For answer, Fernandez moved to one side, and actually took a hand away from the drainpipe. He hung there, standing on one leg, holding on to the drainpipe with one hand, and took something from his pocket. The light shone on the dull grey of a gun.

"Fernandez, get back into the room, or—"

Dawlish saw the gun move round towards him, and backed away when he knew he was covered. The shot hissed out, and a bullet smashed into the window. It was an air-pistol; but could be deadly at close quarters.

Glass cracked and splintered, and Alice cried out from the hall.

Dawlish didn't go back into the line of fire, but turned towards the hall. He met Felicity as he reached the door.

"Pat—" she was pleading.

"I'll stop him outside," Dawlish said brusquely. "Mind, my sweet."

"Let him go!" Felicity cried. "Let him go!" She clutched his arm. "He'll kill you as lief as look at you."

"Darling, don't be crazy." Dawlish tried to tug himself free, but Felicity held on, putting both arms round his neck. Alice dithered, and outside, Fernandez was climbing down the drainpipe. For a split second, Dawlish felt angry—not just exasperated but furiously angry. He took Felicity's wrists and tugged at them, forced her to free her hold, then saw the look which sprang into her eyes.

"Sorry, sweet, but—"

"All right," she said abruptly, and let him go.

She turned away, as if hurt more than words could say. He hesitated. Alice gaped.

Dawlish knew that he was probably too late already, it would probably be a waste of time going down. He oughtn't to have wrenched Felicity's arms away like that.

"Darling—"

"Oh, go and get yourself shot and killed!" she cried.

A few minutes earlier he had been telling himself that nothing would go wrong between them now.

He hurried to the door, hesitated again, glanced round at her—and caught his breath. She was *laughing*. She knew that he would be too late, that she'd won. He grinned and shook his fist at her, then opened the door and ran out.

The house was quiet.

The street was quiet.

Dawlish's car stood outside, gleaming in the street lights, but he didn't need it. There was an empty plot alongside the house, and he raced across this, reaching the back of the plot from where he could see the back of his house and, glancing upwards, the light streaming from the kitchen and the study. A dark head was outlined against the study window, and he saw Felicity wave.

Fernandez had gone; there was no sound except the distant murmur of traffic.

It took Dawlish twenty minutes to get the door open; a chair had been lodged against the handle. A table was on its side, but nothing was missing.

"Darling," Felicity said.

"Yes, *honey.*"

"Precious, I wasn't going to let you run into a bullet from a madman," Felicity reasoned, "even if it was only from an airgun."

"Thank you, sweetheart."

"Fernandez might have done anything."

"Yes, dear."

"But even I know that nothing in the world could keep you out of this for long," Felicity said, philosophically. "Patrick Dawlish the Great Detective couldn't possibly allow himself to be left out in the cold when his name's been taken in vain and when his reputation is besmirched, his honesty questioned and his honour confounded. And—"

"Soon," said Dawlish, "I shall begin to think that you think I did marry the girl."

"I'm suspending judgment." Felicity, leaning back in her winged armchair, looked at him through her lashes. "The question is, what are you going to do first?"

He did not answer at once.

It was half-past eleven.

Alice, still nervous, had been gone for some time. She would have been much more nervous had she known that with Dawlish violence and gunplay were almost occupational risks. There had been no difficulty in persuading her not to talk about it, and they knew her well enough to believe that she would not.

The neighbours had either not heard or not been worried about the breaking glass.

No one had telephoned or called since Fernandez had gone.

He had not rifled the safe or damaged any of the furniture in the study; he had simply opened the window, and in doing so, apparently, had knocked over a table. That had caused the crash.

Now all was quiet, as if a fierce storm had blown itself out.

"Let's hear more about Mepita," Dawlish invited. "Exactly what did she say?"

Felicity shrugged her shoulders hopelessly.

"It was fantastic! She was so pretty—lovely—and happy, too. I—don't grin!—I was almost convinced that you'd fallen for her, but when I heard about a so-called marriage I just had to see what I could find out. But she wouldn't say much. She only stayed for ten minutes or so, because she had an appointment. She—"

Felicity broke off.

"Go on, sweet," murmured Dawlish.

"She sent her love," Felicity said.

Dawlish exploded.

"That's no way of going on," Felicity said. "I'll tell you what you ought to do. Telephone Bill Trivett at his flat, now, and tell him all about it. Fernandez isn't any danger at the moment, and as he's not here you can't blackmail him into talking."

"Granted," Dawlish murmured, "but he might turn up again. I'd like to know why he's nervous of the police."

"Darling, you're slipping." Felicity was still flippant. "The jools he talked about are stolen. It was a skilfully hatched plot, as they thought. Fernandez and his sweet sister stole the jewels, and thought they had pulled off a great coup when the illustrious Mr. Dawlish married into the family. They had to get him married, and then persuade him to handle the stolen gems. The plot," said Felicity firmly, "is so obvious that I can't understand how you failed to see it from the beginning."

"I don't think I'll tell Trivett or anyone else tonight," Dawlish said, compassionately making no comment. "Fernandez may come again. He'll realize that he won't get Mepita by putting a pellet in my head, so he's likely to be in a more reasonable frame of mind in the morning. Let's sleep on it, anyhow."

Felicity's eyes opened wider, and she smiled without any pretence.

"It's been a complete waste of time arguing," she said in a calmer voice. "You know exactly what you want to do, and you always get your own way, don't you? I ought to know by now. Ever since I've known you, you've always taken reckless chances, and you've almost seemed compelled to do things on your own. Most of the time I hate it, because of the risk—but at heart I suppose I wouldn't have you any different."

Dawlish went across to her.

"Thank you, my darling," he said.

He woke early next morning.

Felicity, in the bed nearer the window, was asleep, facing him. She was relaxed, with her medium-coloured hair spread about the pillow; good to see. Her breathing was soft and gentle, and he could just discern the rise and fall of her breast. He smiled faintly, and remembered what she had said last thing.

He had a bent for detection; in a weak moment that brilliant policeman, Trivett of the Yard, had said that he would rather have Dawlish on his side than six trained detectives. It was as if Dawlish could smell crime, and crooks; and sniff his way through mysteries. In the course of his amateur sleuthing—as well as a long spell with M.I.5—he had learned peculiar things. He was able to force almost any lock, open any safe, be ready to take any risk, to match his wits against the police and the crooks.

When he heard about this affair, Trivett of Scotland Yard would expect him to investigate off his own bat; and why not? Insurance companies had been known to ask for his help; private individuals often sought it. There was a kind of twilight world of people who preferred not to let the police handle their affairs.

Those whom he judged worthy, or ill-treated by the Fates, or even unjustly accused, Dawlish was likely to help.

The business at *Gale's* had kept him out of this half-world for some time. He was glad, in a way, to be back in it.

There would be the inevitable bodeful warnings from Trivett, the advice to leave this affair to the police, but . . .

Forget Trivett.

Was anyone impersonating him, Patrick Dawlish? If so, why? How much of Fernandez's story had been genuine? Was there any reason why he and the girl Mepita should make the story up?

"I don't see one," Dawlish said to himself, and got out of bed. Felicity stirred but did not wake. Dawlish went into the bathroom, bathed and shaved, and then put on a kettle for tea. There was something pleasant about being on their own, without a maid living in. Changing social habits had their advantages. But Alice would almost certainly be here in time to cook breakfast.

If he'd heard nothing more by ten o'clock, he decided that he would telephone Trivett at the Yard.

At a quarter-past nine, the telephone rang.

Dawlish looked up from toast and marmalade, Felicity put down her coffee. Dawlish went to the telephone extension in the hall, aware that Felicity had shifted her chair so that she would see him.

"Patrick Dawlish here," Dawlish said; and prepared to deal gently but firmly with Carlos de Ciento y Fernandez.

"Is that Mr. Dawlish's flat?" a girl asked.

"Yes."

"*Daily Record* here, hold on, please," the girl said. "Mr. Allison wants you."

Allison of the *Record* was a friend, and few weeks went by

without their meeting. The call might mean little, was probably just 'hello'.

"It's Allison," Dawlish called to Felicity, and then Allison came to the line.

"Hallo, Pat, you still at liberty?" he asked. "I heard a rumour that you were about to be put in irons and carried off to cells at Scotland Yard, so I wanted to ask Felicity what you'd been up to. But you'll do—any idea why Trivett and the Yard are breathing fire against you—why there's talk that you'll be spending the night in a dungeon?"

He stopped.

Dawlish felt himself turn cold.

CHAPTER V

BLAST FROM TRIVETT

Allison might exaggerate, but Allison would not lie. Dawlish found the thought of Fernandez fading from his mind. Instead, he pictured Trivett when the Yard man thought that he, Dawlish, had abused the unofficial privileges so often granted him. There was, Trivett would say, a line. If Dawlish hadn't the sense—in some moods Trivett would say decency—to keep on the right side of it, then Dawlish would have to suffer for his folly.

Trivett was obviously in such a mood. It was going to be a trying morning.

"I haven't the faintest idea what this is about," Dawlish said.

"Oh, come," protested Allison. "Trivett's the grizzly bear with a sore head, so sore that he's on the rampage. My spies say he hasn't been in a mood like this for years and years and years."

"I still don't know what's worrying him," Dawlish said firmly. "As a matter of fact, I want a chat with him myself."

"You won't get a word in edgeways," Allison warned, and added hopefully: "Anything in this for me?"

"I don't know what it is yet," Dawlish answered promptly,

"but if you're lazing about at the office, there is one little job you could do for me."

"Ah-*ha*," breathed Allison. "The conspirators."

Dawlish could be very patient.

"This is off the record and strictly confidential; if a sentence gets in your misbegotten news-sheet I'll never give you a story again. Find out what you can about a Carlos de Ciento y Fernandez—"

"Whoa back!" There was a busy pause. "I got the Carlos," Allison declared brightly, "you'd better spell the rest."

Dawlish spelt it; and added:

"He has a sister named Mepita. Age—early twenties, and as beautiful as you'd expect. I—"

He heard footsteps on the stairs; deliberate footsteps, which warned him in a moment that Trivett was coming; Trivett, or his myrmidons. There were at least two men, and he judged them to be half-way up the second flight of stairs. He didn't like any of this.

"You were saying," said Allison, invitingly.

"We're in a hurry, Trivett's almost here," Dawlish said. "Find out if the Spanish pair reached London Airport yesterday morning, if they're known at the Embassy—get anything you can. They live—or the man lives—in Barcelona. And remember, you're under oath not to say a word."

"And you told me that Trivett hadn't any cause to be cross," said Allison reprovingly. "See you in the lock-up. Er—Pat—"

The footsteps reached the landing, now; Felicity was moving towards the front door.

"Hurry, oaf," urged Dawlish.

"Supposing the police do hold you, what shall I do with any dope I get about this chap and the girl?" asked Allison. "Tell Felicity and Tim Jeremy?"

Dawlish said:

"Tell Felicity, will you? Tim's abroad."

"You know, they've caught you at a bad time," Allison said with gloomy relish. "Your old reliables, Tim Jeremy and Ted Beresford, both out of the country—no troops you can alert. You'd better be careful."

"I'll be careful."

"Okay," said Allison. "'Bye, old chap, get a good lawyer."

He rang off.

He was a sound man, and no fool. He knew Dawlish well, and also knew those friends of Dawlish he had mentioned—men who had helped to put Dawlish in the headlines and build his almost legendary reputation. They were not handy. Tim Jeremy was due back in England in a few days, but was now touring France, there was no way to get in touch with him.

Allison had said, obliquely, that he thought Dawlish needed his friends about him.

A sharp ring at the front door interrupted Dawlish's gloomy thoughts. Felicity was by his side, but she didn't open the door. Dawlish's manner told her that all was not as pretty as it could be. He looked at her, without thinking about her. Allison was quite sure that real trouble was on the way, or he wouldn't have asked that last question. A case which could present him with a sweet young bigamous wife could produce anything.

The bell rang again.

"What—" began Felicity.

"Trivett," Dawlish answered, and forced himself to grin. "Allison seems to think that trouble's on the wing." He stretched out to open the door. "You wanted me to call Trivett last night, didn't you?"

Felicity didn't answer.

Dawlish opened the door.

It wasn't Trivett, but two large men, one of whom he recognized as a detective sergeant at Scotland Yard; a Sergeant Popple, brick-red of countenance, with small blue eyes and a beat-duty manner.

The two men stood facing Dawlish, who did his best to look as if he were pleased to see them; an amiable giant.

"Good morning," he said brightly.

"Are you Mr. Dawlish?" asked Sergeant Popple.

"Don't tell me your eyesight isn't so good," Dawlish said sadly, but his heart was thumping most uncomfortably, and he sensed what Felicity was feeling.

"Mr. *Patrick* Dawlish," Popple said, "it is my duty to arrest you for receiving stolen jewels, in particular the Kroo emeralds, and I must warn you that anything you say may be used in evidence."

It was like a blow in the face.

It was crazy.

Felicity caught her breath. "Pat!"

Alice was in the kitchen doorway. "*Lumme!*" she gasped and for emphasis: "*Coo!*"

Then Dawlish forced himself to stir.

"That's a bit abrupt," he said, "and nonsense, too. I don't know a thing about the theft or whereabouts of the Kroo emeralds." He turned to Felicity. His eyes told her that was true. "They'll soon find out that it's a mistake," he said, and hoped he sounded carefree. "Stay here until I'm back or I telephone."

Felicity said, "All right," very quietly.

Popple and the other massive detective looked as if they were relieved that Dawlish was going quietly. They had certainly come prepared for trouble. Two more men were in the street, and there was also one at each corner.

They had meant to make quite sure that Dawlish could not get away.

They must have a lot of evidence to act this way. It was still unbelievable. Trivett was a *friend*. Remember that. He might get annoyed, affronted, impatient, even furious; but this was formal arrest, and the police needed evidence that they could make stand up.

Dawlish sat hugely next to Popple in the back of the police car. Popple's shoulder pressed against his. Popple didn't exactly threaten to use handcuffs, but had made it clear that he carried a pair.

Dawlish was not even thinking of escape.

This made no sense at all.

Allison had been prophetic.

Dawlish sat on an upright chair in a cell at Cannon Row, the police station which was just across the way from Scotland Yard. He had been there for an hour. There had been a few formalities, then he had been locked in. No one had come to see him since.

A picture of Fernandez kept coming into his mind's eye; was this to do with the same case?

Of course it was.

But . . .

He stopped trying to answer the question.

He heard footsteps and voices, one of them familiar—Trivett's. Trivett had a deep voice, a military kind of voice, and a military walk. He came along the corridor with Popple and another man. The bars of Dawlish's cell were alongside the passage. Trivett glanced at Dawlish, and then quickly away.

Dawlish liked it much, much less.

Trivett was a friend, remember. He didn't like what he had done and what he was doing, but hadn't given sentiment any slightest chance to play a part. If he were acting on instructions from a superior, he couldn't help himself, of course.

His expression seemed to condemn. He was nearly six feet tall, a lean but well-built man dressed in a dark grey suit of excellent cut. He was handsome, too, in a dark, trim way.

He passed out of sight.

Keys clinked.

Trivett came back with the sergeant on duty, who was rattling the keys. He unlocked the cell, and Trivett and Popple came in, while the other plainclothes man from the Yard stood just outside the cell. The door was closed and locked again—the kind of precaution that would be taken with a dangerous prisoner.

Trivett looked straight into Dawlish's eyes.

"Well, Dawlish," he said heavily.

Dawlish could refuse to take him and all this seriously; could take him seriously and be reproachful; or could take him seriously and get on a high horse. He took a stand half-way between the first two, and hoped for the best.

"Hallo, William," he said; "how long will it take you to put this little blunder right?"

Trivett said: "You know the charge, and you know that you haven't a chance of ducking it."

"William," said Dawlish sadly, "you haven't a ghost of a chance of making it stick." At least, Trivett shouldn't have; but the unmistakable and alarming thing was Trivett's absolute confidence that he could.

It wasn't so easy to keep bright and amiable.

"Why waste our time?" Trivett growled. He took out cigarettes and offered them; his first concession. He lit up, and gave Dawlish a light. "I'm not going to waste time. Anyhow, I don't give a damn why you bought the emeralds. I only know you did."

"Wrong," Dawlish said, and was glad of the cigarette.

Trivett said: "Listen, we've got the emeralds from the shop—from *Gale's.* And we've got Pratt."

They'd found the emeralds at *Gale's*; stolen gems. They wouldn't lie about it. That was like another blow in the face, and it helped to explain Trivett's harshness.

It was crazy.

And Pratt? Who was he?

Vaguely, Dawlish recalled hearing of someone named Pratt; but it was not the sensation which Trivett obviously expected it to be. Trivett obviously thought that once Dawlish knew that 'Pratt' was under arrest, he would know that the game was up. At sight of Dawlish's blank face, Trivett showed animation for the first time—a frown. He barked:

"D'you hear? We've got Pratt."

"And who," asked Dawlish, "is Pratt? Pratt, Pratt, Pratt—let me see?" He frowned, in turn, and then he smiled as if inspired. "Oh, yes, there's a Pratt on the staff of the *Echo,* that's the chap I'm thinking of."

Trivett said: "Tiny Pratt."

"Sorry," said Dawlish, beginning to feel better. "I don't know his nickname."

"Are you trying to tell me that you don't know Tiny Pratt?" demanded Trivett, and shot a glance at Popple. That also did Dawlish little good, for Popple only looked sceptical. Unlike Trivett, he would hope to make this charge stick.

"He knows him all right," said Popple nastily.

"If I know him, it's not by the name of Pratt," said Dawlish, and decided that this was the moment to pretend that he was not perturbed. It was also the first moment in which he felt almost cheerful. "Don't keep me too long, Bill, I've still a lot to do. You nearly had a call last night, but I wouldn't disturb you at home."

Trivett said: "What about?"

"An odd business. Yesterday afternoon a lovely luscious Spanish lass turned up at the flat and introduced herself to Fel as my wife." He saw Trivett start, and that did him still more good. "The pretty went off, and during the evening her brother turned up. He seemed most annoyed when I pointed out that I'd been married to Felicity for—"

Dawlish stopped.

Trivett's face was beginning to show bewilderment; and Popple appeared to take more serious interest.

"—so long," Dawlish went on hastily, anxious to take the fullest possible advantage of this improvement in the atmosphere. "So some villain has been impersonating me. There was a rigmarole about stolen jewels, too, but I didn't know a thing about that. What's this story about Tiny Pratt and the Kroo emeralds at the shop?" he added with deceitful casualness. "Do you seriously think I bought them from the thief?"

"That's it," Trivett said. He schooled himself to behave more like a senior officer at Scotland Yard than a man who had been knocked completely off his perch. "You wait here," he added grimly. "We'll soon settle this." He turned abruptly, and the duty sergeant unlocked the door. "I don't care how long it takes," Trivett went on. "I want eight or nine men of about Dawlish's height and colouring here, so that we can line him up with them. Then we'll see."

He glowered and disappeared.

The cell door clanged and the key turned in the lock.

Dawlish drew on the half-finished cigarette and faced the fact that before long he would take part in an identification parade.

CHAPTER VI

PARADE

Dawlish heard men's footsteps again.

Nearly an hour had passed since Trivett had left, and it had not been a comfortable time. The finding of the stolen jewels at *Gale's* was bad; the kind of thing which would compel Trivett to act like this. And mistakes could be made on identification parades. Probably Trivett was going to ask the unknown Tiny Pratt to pick out the man to whom he had sold the emeralds—and there was a possibility that Pratt would deliberately pick out Dawlish. This was a clever conspiracy on the part of whoever was impersonating him, and Pratt might be in the know.

There was little relief; and he felt worse because he guessed what Felicity would be thinking and feeling.

The Fernandez affair was part of the same pattern. There had been no warning, no time to prepare his mind, no time to plan a defence. Fighting the unknown was always unnerving, and he couldn't be sure that there would be a chance to fight.

Pratt was a jewel thief.

Pratt might name Dawlish to disaster.

But why? What was this plot about?

The men walked towards the cell, and passed; Trivett wasn't one of them, but Dawlish heard his own name mentioned. The keys clinked again.

They came back, and opened the cell door.

"Come with us, Mr. Dawlish, please," said Popple, and led the way. Dawlish walked briskly into the yard. Eight or nine men were moving about, most of them dressed in raincoats and all bareheaded. There were vague similarities; they were big, within an inch or two of one another in height, and none was really fat or really thin; all were more fair than dark, too, but there the likenesses ended.

Trivett was standing by with another Yard man.

It was a warm June day, but Dawlish felt shivery.

Popple took a raincoat from a uniformed policeman and handed it to Dawlish.

"Put that on, please."

Dawlish obeyed.

Trivett was watching, but Trivett was cold and aloof, showing no sign of friendliness; that suggested that he was still half convinced that Dawlish was the wanted man.

"Now, gentlemen, *if* you please," Popple said to the other big men standing about, somewhat self-consciously, "I'll be glad if you'll line up along here." He pointed to the wall. "The middle position, please," he added, and Dawlish joined the others. All of these stared at him as at a pariah dog, knowing that he was the prisoner. The rest had been picked off the streets by men of the Yard and Cannon Row, to touch Dawlish's life for ten minutes or so; and then to vanish.

There were nine—and he was in the middle, standing with his back to a high, grey wall of the police station. They stood there for several minutes, until a man was brought into the yard. 'Tiny' was a nickname meant quite literally. The newcomer wasn't five feet tall, and he was very thin. He walked with a slight limp, throwing his left foot forward. His head was a little on one side, giving him the impression of being deformed. He looked up from beneath his brows, and his eyes were large and expressive. He had thin features and a nose with a pale, shiny, narrow tip.

He came limping across, with massive policemen on either side of him.

He joined Trivett, and peered up at him.

"You know what you're to do, Tiny," Trivett said, "and don't make any mistakes. If you give the right man a miss, it will go harder with you."

"Don't you worry, Mr. Trivett," said Tiny Pratt, in a voice so deep that it startled the nine men and made them look at him sharply. It was quite a pleasant voice, too. "I'll put a finger on Dawlish, don't worry at all."

Dawlish felt his mouth go dry.

The attention of all the other men was now on Tiny Pratt.

Tiny was slightly in advance of his captors as he walked along the line of men. He moved slowly. His head was bent downwards all the time, and he had to look up—it was a slight natural deformity.

He had a bright face at close quarters and his eyes were very clear. He wasn't a man to dislike on sight. He did not pause in that first inspection, and seemed to spend exactly the same time looking at each man.

Dawlish's heart began to thump.

"May I see them again?" asked Pratt, heartily.

"Take your time," Trivett said.

They began again. This time, Pratt's gaze lingered on each face. Dawlish felt the gaze of the bright blue eyes on him; the little man seemed to stare at him longer than he stared at anyone. Imagination? He felt as if he were suffocating.

They passed.

An age seemed to pass, too.

Pratt reached the end of the line again. Each man in it seemed touched by uneasiness, as if the shadow of guilt were on them all. The sun shone brightly on the rest of the yard, but the wall kept it off them.

"May I—*once* more?" asked Pratt, earnestly.

"Yes," said Trivett.

Pratt began that limping walk again, and this time he passed the first three men with hardly a glance but stopped at one next to Dawlish. Dawlish knew why; the man was more like him than anyone else in the line. Pratt scrutinized the other's face intently—and then, without moving, glanced at Dawlish.

He didn't look away.

Dawlish felt his cheeks going pale; felt as if the finger of the little man was going to point towards him; had he been guilty, he could not have felt much worse. Pratt wasn't allowed to point, though; would have to identify his man afterwards.

Then Pratt walked on.

Would he name Dawlish?

Dawlish gulped as he breathed.

Pratt stopped at the end man but one—and Dawlish knew why; that man also bore a fairly close resemblance to him. Pratt was looking for someone very like him, so the ordeal wasn't yet over.

"Well, which one was it?" asked Trivett, in a rough voice.

"To tell you the truth," Tiny Pratt said, "he isn't here at all."

Although he was out of earshot, that was the moment when the whole outlook changed for Dawlish; when he was able to face life, the future, Felicity, Trivett, and the whole wide world with cheerfulness which made life worth living.

Pratt was in earnest; and he looked worried. Now, he turned his face round and twisted his head so that he could look into Trivett's eyes. They were in a corner of the courtyard.

"I know you'll think I'm lying, Mr. Trivett, but the fellow just isn't here. He has smaller eyes than any one of these *and* a little scar in his chin. Just—there." Pratt touched his own chin a little to the right of centre. "It's no use lying to you, is it, even if I can't give you what you want."

"That's all right, Tiny." Trivett was brisk but not unfriendly. In fact he was tremendously relieved. "I'll see you again soon." He nodded, and Pratt was taken off by two policemen, and Trivett joined the men who had lined-up. "Thank you very much, gentlemen," he said to the others, "I'm most grateful for your help. Glad no one identified one of you as a rogue!"

He won a laugh—as he must have won hundreds at the end of identification parades.

The men dispersed, talking.

Trivett, a different Trivett who looked as if he had a weight off his shoulders, actually grinned at Dawlish.

"You probably fixed Tiny to talk about a man with a scar and smaller eyes," he said, "but it looks as if there could be some mistake. If there is, I can see you're going to have plenty to do. I'll see you in the office—mind he doesn't run away from you, Popple."

Popple forced a smile. He didn't utter any protest, but obviously he wasn't satisfied.

"No, Pratt didn't pick Dawlish out, sir," Trivett said to the Assistant Commissioner of the C.I.D. "We could hold Dawlish because the Kroo emeralds were found at *Gale's,* but he's not the only one with a key. There are several members of the staff who could be involved."

The A.C. said: "What do you want to do?"

"Give Dawlish plenty of rope," said Trivett. "Let him know we can pick him up any time, and see what happens."

There was a pause. Then:

"Oh, all right," growled the A.C.

Trivett's office was long and narrow, with windows along one wall overlooking the Embankment and the Thames, and the branches of plane trees so close to the window that a man could stretch out a hand and pluck leaves; and when the sun was on the other side of the river the trees cast shadows into the room.

The walls were distempered cream. There were a few photographs of dead and gone panjandrums at the Yard, looking very Victorian and bewhiskered, and two of cricket elevens. One desk was at the far end of the room, away from the door and near the fireplace. This was Trivett's. At the other end was a smaller desk, used by his chief aide, Chief Inspector Pell.

Pell wasn't there.

Trivett was positively bustling in his geniality.

"Sit down, Pat . . . Cigarette?" They lit up, and Dawlish dropped into a comfortable armchair. Trivett sat on the corner of his desk, swinging a leg. "You have the luck," he declared. "If Pratt had identified you, it would have sent you down for a stretch. As it is, I'm not sure that I shouldn't hold you. Those emeralds were found in a drawer in *Gale's*. Pratt said he'd sold them to you, so we got a search warrant. You're free—for the time being—because of one thing only."

"What's that?"

"Your prints aren't on the case the jewels are in," Trivett said. "Tiny Pratt lifted the Kroo emeralds—didn't you read about the burglary?"

"I remember now."

"They were nice gems, but nothing really special," Trivett told him. "A neat job, rather like all of Tiny's—he's been inside once. One of the few thieves I've ever liked as an individual," Trivett went on, briskly. "Almost honest in some ways. We picked him up, as he'd left a dab. He wouldn't say a word, but his wife had heard him talking about selling to Dawlish—and he admitted it when we named you."

Trivett stopped.

Dawlish said: "Go on, Bill," very softly.

"So we searched *Gale's*. When we found the emeralds, we took it for granted that you'd slipped up trying to help a client, if client's the word," Trivett went on. "It looked a simple case, open and shut, but if Pratt swears you aren't the man—how did you fix him?"

Dawlish grinned.

"I've never seen him in my life before!"

"All right, all right," growled Trivett. "If I find that the pair of you have fooled me, you'll know all about it. Now, I've some other questions—"

"Easy," Dawlish protested. "Mind if I start thinking? Pratt didn't sell to me—so who did he sell to?"

"Someone calling himself Patrick Dawlish," Trivett answered quietly. "Like the man you were talking about, who married a Spanish girl." Trivett lit a cigarette from the stub of the one he was smoking, then put the stub out. "A matter of impersonation, apparently, but we can go into that when we get all the rest squared up. Give me an account of your movements on the evening of May 9th, will you?"

Dawlish cast his mind back. . . .

Felicity's eyes were bright, she found it easy to smile, but she didn't find it easy to hide the fact that she had been through a bad few hours.

Dawlish was back at the flat. He told her what had happened, and:

"It wouldn't have been too good, sweetheart. On May 9th, when I was supposed to have taken the emeralds from Pratt, you and I were on our own here," he said. "Proving it wouldn't have been so simple. But when everything was added up, Trivett decided that it may be a genuine case of an impersonation. He gave me a break, anyhow—he probably thinks I'm doing a job for a client he doesn't know." Dawlish felt as if clean invigorating winds were blowing; the problem was now just a problem to be solved. "And a job for me!"

"Did you tell him about Fernandez?"

"Nearly everything," Dawlish murmured. "I forgot to tell him that Fernandez wasn't happy about consulting the police. Oh, memory, where is thy knotted handkerchief? And I also struck a bargain." He smiled reminiscently at Trivett's willingness to co-operate; a willingness that must have been approved by the Powers-That-Were at the Yard. "The Yard isn't going to do anything about Fernandez until I say go. The jewels Fernandez talked about might be the Kroo emeralds, of course—we'll find out. I wish I knew where to find Fernandez. Perhaps Allison has picked something up." He paused and went on thoughtfully: "Fernandez hasn't telephoned?"

Felicity said: "No."

Dawlish didn't speak.

Felicity said slowly: "I've been so full of our own worries I haven't really thought about that girl's. Where is she? Whom *did* she marry? Was it a genuine marriage, or just a form, so that the man could get his hands on her jewels?"

"Questions by the dozen," Dawlish agreed, "and we don't

know any of the answers. Just at the moment there's one I'd like to know more than the rest."

He looked grim. He looked dangerous. Felicity recognized all the signs, knew that he'd recovered from the day's shock, but was now beginning to feel sore about it; even vengeful.

"You mean, who's using your name?" suggested Felicity.

"I mean, where is Mepita Fernandez?" Dawlish said softly, "and if it comes to that, where's Carlos? I wonder if Allison has any news."

He moved across the study towards the telephone.

It rang as he reached it.

"Patrick Dawlish here," he said into the mouthpiece.

"Mr. Dawlish," said Fernandez in a voice which sounded as if he were being hounded by a thousand demons, "I cannot come to see you, but—will you *please* come to see me?"

CHAPTER VII

APPOINTMENT

Dawlish had heard such heartrending appeals as that before. Any actor could make one. This had all the hallmarks of an outmoded trick—but the voice sounded like the Spaniard's, and there would be nothing surprising about an emergency.

"Where are you?" asked Dawlish, and motioned to Felicity. She hurried to the extension telephone in the hall.

"Please, come here," Fernandez said jerkily. "I am in my hotel, at the Cromwell Road, the Litton Hotel, *Lit-ton*. I must stay and I must talk to you. I am sorry about last night, I was too hasty. Please—"

"All right," Dawlish said abruptly. "I'll come."

"Please!" cried Fernandez. "Hurry."

He rang off.

Dawlish put down the receiver as Felicity came hurrying from the hall—Felicity with a lot on her mind and a stormy look in her lovely eyes.

"Pat—"

"The Litton Hotel, Cromwell Road," Dawlish mused, "they aren't exactly staying at Savoy level, are they?"

"It might not have been Fernandez."

"I couldn't agree more, but it probably was."

"You're not to go there alone."

"We're almost identical twins this morning," Dawlish said, and hugged her. "I'll get Allison to come with me. I shall not take you, you've got to go and take pictures of handsome young Guards officers who make passes at you."

"I can put the sitting off."

"Hideous thought for a Guardsman," said Dawlish, "and there's no need to break his heart. I know that I might run into trouble, so I'll be as careful as you would yourself. Go and get the likeness took, but don't go committing bigamy."

"Pat," Felicity said, very slowly, "I'm worried about that Spanish girl. I'm really worried about her. I think that's what affected me most yesterday, she was so—good."

"Good?" Dawlish echoed.

"In the—pure sense," Felicity went on, flushing, "and don't laugh at me!"

"It's the last thing I'd do," Dawlish said, and then the telephone bell rang again. He answered it, and Felicity made no attempt to get to the extension. If she thought that about Mepita, then she was probably right.

It was Allison.

"I've a little dope," the newspaperman said, "but nothing that makes Fernandez a villain. Like it over lunch, Pat? The *Record* owes you a meal, I think, and I know a spot—"

"At the corner of Cromwell Road, this end, in twenty minutes," Dawlish said. "We'll worry about lunch afterwards."

He did not take the Humber, because it would be too noticeable. He hired an Austin A-40 from the garage which did all his service work, and in twenty-five minutes he was at the corner of

Cromwell Road. The sun shone almost directly overhead, and upon the dark curls of the newspaperman, who stood at the corner, looking up and down, his round face a picture of restful innocence. Allison looked more like an impudent choir boy or a student priest than one of the most experienced and toughened crime reporters on Fleet Street.

Dawlish in the Austin surprised him.

"Why, hallo," he said. "Coming down in the world?"

"There's no profit in business any longer, we're going back to pigs," Dawlish mourned. "Hop in."

Allison climbed in.

"What is all this?"

Dawlish said: "We can go into the details later. Any news from the airport?"

"The male Fernandez arrived first, the sister, Mepita, some hours afterwards."

"Sure?"

"Yes."

"Thanks," said Dawlish. "Now I'll tell you why we're here."

He turned into Cromwell Road and drove towards the Litton Hotel, which he had discovered was on the left-hand side and about halfway down. The houses were all alike, tall, grey, most of them freshly painted. Over the porches of most was a legend— the So-and-So Hotel. A few were offices and commercial studios.

There was little traffic in the wide road.

Dawlish looked about him, and kept an eye on the mirror, but did not seem to be followed.

He slowed down, and as he neared the Litton Hotel took a gun out of the dashboard pocket and slipped it into his coat. That told Allison he took the case seriously. He had not told the police about the message from the Spaniard; he did not think that Fernandez would talk freely to the police.

The bright sun made even the street seem gay.

A man was walking along the pavement, away from them. Dawlish noticed him because one minute he had been standing at a gateway, with a newspaper in his hand, the next, he seemed to be in a hurry to get away. He wore a shabby-looking light grey suit, a trilby hat, and down-at-heel shoes, and he walked in a way that was vaguely familiar.

Dawlish drove past him.

The man stared straight ahead, without glancing at the car; there was no reason why he should. His head was down a little, as if he were brooding even as he walked. He wore thick-lensed glasses.

Dawlish said softly: "Well, well. Like a job, Ally?"

"Oh, no. There's a story in this, and it's mine."

"Follow that chap, and you'll get a better."

"My dear Pat—"

"I'm not fobbing you off," Dawlish assured him, "he was in Withy Street last night."

Allison said brightly, "I'll fix him," and seemed quite happy to leave Dawlish to visit Fernandez alone.

Dawlish turned the first corner to the left, and Allison jumped out. Before the man with the thick-lensed glasses reached the corner Dawlish was a long way off in the car, and Allison was walking towards the Cromwell Road.

Dawlish took two left turns, to reach Cromwell Road again. He was fifty yards from the Litton Hotel. He left the car at the side of the road and walked briskly towards the hotel. Allison was some way off, a few yards behind the man with the thick-lensed glasses.

Dawlish turned into the hotel, and reached a narrow hallway. A bell-push by the side of a frosted glass window said: *Ring.* He didn't ring. The hall was pleasantly furnished, and a flight of stairs, carpeted from banisters to wall, faced him.

There was no sound.

He took a pen-knife from his pocket and opened a blade upon which Trivett would have looked with suspicion. He prised up the fronted glass window, which gave no trouble. Beyond was a cubicle of an office, with a counter, filing cabinets, telephones, all the usual oddments—and a big ledger, open and with the word *Register* at the top.

Dawlish turned this round, and scanned the entries. Two people had come in that day, several on the previous day, and among them was:

Carlos de Ciento y Fernandez

The signature was bold and the letters well-formed, although by English standards ornate and too full of flourishes. Opposite it was the room number, 17.

Mepita hadn't registered here.

Dawlish closed the book and the window.

No one stirred.

He reached the stairs, and saw another flight, leading downwards towards a semi-basement, with a sign *Dining Room* pointing towards this. So the guests were at lunch. He didn't go down to see if Fernandez was with the others, but hurried up the stairs. The carpet deadened all sound of his footsteps.

At the first landing, he saw two passages, one in each direction. Several houses had been made into one, by the simple expedient of knocking down the walls at the end of the passage. Large white-painted doors led off each passage. He saw the first number, 3. He walked right and then left; the highest number here was 14.

He went up the next flight of stairs.

There was still no sound.

Number 17 was at the end of a passage. He hesitated outside it, trying to get its position clear in his mind. It overlooked the back yard of the hotel. Not Cromwell Road. He bent down and put his eye to the keyhole. All he could see was a stretch of green carpet and a piece of furniture which glistened in the sun.

There was no sound anywhere.

He tapped, very softly.

If Fernandez was in there, waiting for him, he would hear that; but if he was in the dining-room, Dawlish would have a chance to turn round.

There was no answer.

He rapped again, more loudly but still quietly. He heard a sound some way off—footsteps on the stairs, and someone breathing heavily. There was a door marked *Maid's Pantry*. He stepped inside this, among the smell of clean linen and soap. He peered out, and saw a woman reach the head of the stairs, a very fat, spreading woman in a blue cotton frock that was too tight for her. She was breathing asthmatically, and looked hot and distressed.

She turned to the right, along the other passage.

Dawlish waited until she had gone into a room, and then approached Fernandez's room again. When there was no response to the third tap, he tried the handle.

The door was locked.

He took out the knife again, and opened it at a blade which would have made Trivett frown even more darkly, for it was, unmistakably, a pick-lock. Trivett, however, was compelled to admit that the police had taught Dawlish all he knew about such nefarious tools, to prepare him for M.I.5.

The lock turned.

Dawlish put the knife back, and opened the door quietly.

He saw a dressing-table near the window, with one drawer open; oddments from it were on the floor. He saw a man's foot by the side of the single bed; the man himself was hidden by the bed. He saw all that in a moment of time, a moment when his mind seemed to stop.

Then he saw the man by the wall flush with the door, hand raised, ugly weapon in it.

The hand was sweeping downwards.

The man was small, and standing on tip-toe, as if to smash the blow on to the top of Dawlish's head. He wore a trilby hat. Except for his eyes, his face was covered with a red silk scarf. The eyes were just eyes, glinting into the bright light which came into the room.

Dawlish backed, swiftly.

The weapon, a length of iron piping, caught him a glancing blow on the shoulder. The man struck again. Dawlish pushed the swinging arm aside, then banged his head against the wall. His ears rang. He felt another blow, then his legs were hooked from under him.

He reeled against the wall.

He saw the little man rushing past along the passage, and heard the thud of his footsteps—but he could do nothing to stop him. He straightened up and turned towards the landing, but by then the man was out of sight; his footsteps sounded clearly as he ran.

Dawlish started forward, and winced.

His head seemed to swell, and the floor seemed to come up and hit him. He would have fallen but for the wall. The sound of running footsteps faded. His ears were still ringing, but gradually other sounds pierced his consciousness—of cars, moving along the road not far away.

That was all.

There was silence again in the hotel. The fat woman did not appear to have been alarmed.

He turned towards the room.

The only part which had not been disturbed was that opposite the door and visible through the keyhole. The rest was in a chaotic state. Nothing had been left untouched, and the mattress had been pulled from the bed and ripped open with a knife. Cushions had been slashed. Two suit-cases, of handsome new leather, were cut beyond repair. Clothes were strewn about the room.

And a man's foot showed at the far side of the bed.

It did not move, but lay limp—just one foot, and a highly-polished brown shoe, the crèpe rubber sole much thicker and wider than the English style; and a wine red sock.

Dawlish went forward, slowly. His head was clearing but he wasn't quite steady, and couldn't hurry.

He was quite sure that he was going to see a dead Fernandez. It was not Fernandez, but he did not think that there was much doubt that the man who lay there was dead.

The victim seemed young. He was well-dressed in brown. His hair was raven black, he had the look of a Spaniard, but no—it was not Fernandez.

His throat was cut.

Blood stained the carpet and his shirt, his collar and tie, but it had come sluggishly and there was not much there, the man *might* be alive.

CHAPTER VIII

VICTIM

There was a telephone in the room.

Dawlish hesitated, moved towards it, then turned towards the injured man. The cut was not deep, and he did not think that it had touched the carotid artery. He loosened his collar and tie and put a pillow beneath the man's head, then piled blankets over him. Then he stepped to the telephone and dialled 999. Soon he was through to the Yard.

"Information Room, Scotland Yard, can I help you?"

"Send an ambulance and a doctor to the Litton Hotel, Cromwell Road," Dawlish said, "Room 17, probably attempted murder."

The man who answered said calmly:

"Yes, sir. Litton Hotel, Room 17."

"That's right."

"Your name, sir, please."

"Dawlish," Dawlish said. "Patrick Dawlish."

Help would be here in a matter of minutes; a police patrol car might come within seconds. He had little time. He rang out a towel, knelt by the man's side and saw that there was a slight movement of the lips. He cleansed the wound, then saw another on the back of the head. He cleaned them both; the bleeding had practically stopped.

He felt inside the man's coat pocket, and drew out a wallet.

There was practically nothing in this: two pound notes, some peseta notes of small denomination which probably meant that the victim had been in Spain recently, a few English stamps, and a postcard-sized photograph of a girl.

Dawlish stared at this.

She was very, very beautiful.

He could not be sure, but he had a feeling that she was Mepita. This girl would impress Felicity; would impress anyone. There was a strange quality of restfulness, of purity, about the girl's expression; a madonna-like saintliness. She was smiling, though, and there was gaiety in her magnificent eyes.

Dawlish hesitated—and then slid the photograph into his pocket, but put the money back.

He heard footsteps, as of men running. The police? He stood up and went to the door. Two men, one of them in police uniform, were approaching; so a patrol car had been near. The other man was in plain clothes. At sight of Dawlish they stopped like puppets at the end of invisible strings.

"In here," Dawlish said.

A third man came hurrying up the stairs.

"I assure you, it's a mistake, we've had no trouble here, officer. We—" he was small, eager, distressed—and when he saw Dawlish, startled.

"Your mistake, I'm afraid," Dawlish said. "It's touch and go, I think."

Dawlish and the police made inquiries, swiftly. Fernandez had gone out before lunch; he hadn't been seen since. His sister—a young woman he had called his sister, anyway—had been to visit him the previous afternoon; she hadn't shown up since.

The injured man had been taken away in an ambulance, with a doctor agreeing with Dawlish that it was touch and go. The police crowded the room. Dawlish stood by the window, looking out over backyards and the backs of houses in the parallel street. No one had asked him more than formal questions.

He wondered where Allison was.

He heard Trivett's voice, and stirred.

"Hallo, Pat," Trivett said, in a tone which was neither hostile nor friendly. "What's all this?"

"Simple," Dawlish answered. "Fernandez called me, and I came to see him. I found the man with his head battered and his throat cut."

"Any idea who'd want to kill Fernandez?"

"No, not the foggiest," said Dawlish. "Only this wasn't Fernandez. It was someone I've never seen before."

"I got this out of his coat pocket," one of the plain-clothes men said, "it's addressed to a Señor Corez." Dawlish hadn't seen this letter. "A *poste restante* address, too—Thomas Cook's," the man added.

"Thanks," Trivett said, and took it. "What did you find in his pocket, Pat?" That was friendlier; that was the tone that Dawlish wanted to hear.

"Nothing," Dawlish answered lightly. "Cross my heart!"

"Sure?"

"Bill," Dawlish said, "I'm on your side. This is mixed up with the impersonation business, and I need help. My troops are away," he added sadly, "or I'd be more independent."

Trivett grinned.

"Did you come here alone?"

"Allison was with me," Dawlish told him, "and he followed a Suspicious Looking Person."

Trivett said: "I wish you idiots would call us right away." He watched the men who were already beginning to take photographs and measurements. Someone had drawn an outline, in chalk, round the wounded man's body; and the measurements were being taken from this. Another man was making a sketch; two others were looking in the rifled drawers. Trivett stubbed out a cigarette that was burned very low, and lit another, as he glanced round.

"All right," he said, "you don't seem to have wasted much time. Tell Allison I'd like a word with him, will you?"

"Yes, gladly."

"And Pat."

"Yes?"

"Don't bite off more than you can chew," Trivett said.

When he was downstairs, and recalling Trivett's parting comment, Dawlish found himself smiling for the first time since he had entered the room. His head ached, and there were bruises there and on his shoulder, but nothing was enough to put him out of action.

He wondered where Allison was, and he soon stopped smiling. What was funny about this job?

What was funny about a man so viciously attacked?

Why had he been attacked?

Where was Fernandez?

Dawlish had given Trivett a full description of the young Spaniard, and there would be a call out for the man soon. But it might not lead anywhere. There was at least a possibility that Fernandez was dead.

His sister, if he had told the truth about that, had been missing since yesterday evening, and a photograph which might be hers was in Dawlish's pocket. If she had been kidnapped, if the men who had attacked Corez held her captive . . .

Why think of her as a prisoner? Why not think of her as a corpse? She had been prevented from coming back to the Withy Street flat. Felicity was in no doubt that she had meant to return; and there had been no apparent reason why she should not. She had planned to meet Fernandez at the flat—again, *if* the youth had told the truth—and she hadn't come.

She would have, had it been possible; so—she had been prevented.

Dawlish looked up and down Cromwell Road. There was more traffic now, most of it moving faster than it should. Two policemen stood outside the hotel, and a crowd of a dozen people had already gathered, men, women and youths. They gaped.

One called:

"What's up, mister?"

"Sorry," said Dawlish, "not my affair." He broke through the crowd, and stepped out briskly towards the hired car. He wondered if Allison would be sitting inside it, but there was no sign of the newspaperman, and he wasn't likely to come back here now.

Dawlish drove off, with another puzzle growing large on his mind.

Where was Allison? What had kept him away for so long? The obvious answers were that he was still following the man with the thick-lensed glasses, but there was no certainty. The girl was missing, Fernandez was missing, Allison . . .

Nonsense!

Dawlish reached Withy Street. Felicity was out, she had been to lunch with a friend, but Alice was in, a spick-and-span Alice, ready for the afternoon, in a navy blue dress and her hair nicely brushed and drawn back from her forehead with a bun at the back. She had scrubbed her face, which glistened and, except for lipstick, was innocent of make-up.

"Think you could find me a snack, Alice?"

"Oh, Mr. Dawlish, don't say you haven't had lunch," said Alice, hurriedly. "You must be *fam*ished. There's a nice bit of cold ham in the frige, though, and a lovely fresh lettuce, I'll have you something in two shakes of a lamb's tail."

She hurried off.

Dawlish went to the window, keeping close to the side, so that he could see out without being seen. A little man was sitting at the wheel of a small car, not far along.

Dawlish studied his face, carefully.

Alice had the meal ready in ten minutes. As she checked that everything needed was on the table, Dawlish took out the girl's photograph.

"Ever seen her before, Alice?"

Alice hardly needed to think.

"Oh, yes, she was here yesterday afternoon, Mr. Dawlish. Isn't she *lovely*?"

"Not bad," agreed Dawlish slowly. "Not bad at all."

So this was a picture of Mepita Fernandez; and the victim of the attack had had it in his pocket.

A girl so beautiful that she could affect Felicity as she had, and win such spontaneous tribute from Alice, must be really lovely in the flesh. She was superb enough in the photograph— and she was missing, remember.

Should he take it to Trivett?

It wasn't always wise to let the Yard know everything. There were ways and means which were denied the police. Dawlish was under suspicion of playing a lone hand; why not justify the suspicion? He hadn't been in that murky half-world of crime for over a year, but he could go back, rely on friends who would not help the Yard. Wasn't this a case where he might get results which the Yard couldn't?

A man calling himself Dawlish, representing himself as Patrick Dawlish of *Gale's,* remember, had bought those stolen emeralds from Tiny Pratt. So, there was a reasonable chance that the impersonator was connected with the attack on the injured Corez; and with the little man who had attacked Dawlish.

Dawlish ate thoughtfully.

He expected a call from Allison, but it did not come.

Alice fussed in with coffee; when he was here alone Alice came very near to pampering him, and he did not discourage her. Today he was hardly aware that she was in the room. He took his coffee into the study, and telephoned the *Daily Record.*

Allison wasn't there, and hadn't called up during the morning: he had left word that he had gone to see Mr. Patrick Dawlish.

"Thanks," Dawlish said, and rang off.

He went to the window; the little man was still in the car.

Dawlish left the flat, whistling, reached the street and was unaware that Alice was watching him from the front-room window. He took the hired Austin and drove to the end of the street, away from the Embankment. The man moved from the car near a house, and walked along Withy Street. Dawlish drove past two streets, then took the next right turning; and in three minutes he was back in the street.

The man who had come from the car was stepping into the house where Dawlish had his flat.

No one else was in sight.

Dawlish left the car at the corner, and ran towards the house, reaching it as he heard a knock at the top flat—his flat. He hurried up the stairs, keeping close to the side, to avoid creaking. The man knocked at his door again; and rang at the same time.

Dawlish reached the first landing.

He heard Alice's voice.

"*Good* afternoon."

"Good afternoon," a man said in a voice which sounded clearly. "Is Mr. Dawlish in?"

"Well, he isn't, he's just gone out," Alice began, while Dawlish crept up the stairs. "If you'd been here three minutes earlier you would—*oh!*" Her voice rose in a scream.

That was all.

Dawlish reached the second landing, then stepped on the next flight of stairs, and could see the man going into his flat. He couldn't see Alice, but he heard her say in shrill alarm:

"Don't—don't hurt me, *please* don't hurt me!"

The man said softly: "Just turn round, sweetie."

"Don't"—a hysterical note sprang to Alice's voice—"don't hurt me!"

"Keep quiet, you little fool, and turn round!"

Alice caught her breath.

Dawlish saw the man's arm raised, as he had seen it raised once before.

He said casually:

"Don't hurt her, will you?"

The little man swung round. Dawlish was already half-way across the landing, automatic in hand. The man flung the piece of iron piping. Dawlish ducked, and it flew over his head, crashed against the wall and clattered down the stairs.

"Stay where—" Dawlish began.

The little man launched himself forward, but didn't get far. Alice shot out a leg and hooked his legs from under him. Then, as if horrified at her own temerity, she stood looking down at him with her mouth wide open, all her teeth showing. The little man seemed stunned for a moment, but began to wriggle, then to squirm.

Dawlish said mildly: "We can't have him acting like this, Alice, can we?" He hauled the man to his feet, twisted his right arm behind him in a hammer lock, and then forced him into the hall. Alice stood with a hand on the door until they were inside, then closed the door and asked squeakily:

"Is there anything else, sir?"

"Just wait in the kitchen, will you?" asked Dawlish, and smiled at her so warmly that her colour returned and she began to blush. "You were very brave indeed." He pushed the little man ahead of him again, and when they were in the study, kicked the door to.

He was quite sure that this was the man from the Litton Hotel; probably the assailant; possibly a murderer.

He let the man go.

"Don't—don't you play any funny tricks with me," the man said in a squeaky voice, "you'll know all about it if you do, Dawlish."

CHAPTER IX

O'FLYNN

"That's right," Dawlish said, "I'll hear about it if I play any tricks with you." He smiled; but it was not a smile which Felicity or Trivett would have recognized. It did not touch his eyes, and his mouth was very tight and thin.

The little man licked his lips, as if something in Dawlish's face frightened him. His clothes were identical with those of the man who had escaped from the Litton Hotel.

"I—I've got too much on you," he muttered, but his voice lacked the note of confidence.

"Far too much," agreed Dawlish, and suddenly shot out a hand and slapped the man on the side of the face. He slapped the other cheek, and sent him reeling backwards. A flare of anger which might easily get out of control flooded over him; he fought it back.

The little man cringed against a chair, lips parted, confidence all gone, fear written large on a face which should have earned him some sympathy.

It was round and very pale, a moon of a face, with small, dark eyes in it, a button of a nose, a large, loose mouth; and damp, almost colourless lips.

"If Corez dies," Dawlish said, "I'll drag you along to Scotland Yard by your hair. Why did you cut his throat?"

The man said: "I—I had—I didn't mean—"

"Stop stalling," Dawlish growled savagely. "Let's have the truth, fast."

The little man muttered: "I was going through the room, see, Fernandez's room, and then this guy turns up. It was him or me, see?" He was almost choking with fear.

"Only he didn't have a cosh."

"It—it was him or me!"

"Who are you, and what's your name?"

"I—I'm Micky O'Flynn." That came spontaneously enough and sounded as if it were the truth. "I pick up what work I can, any kind of job—"

"Burglary, housebreaking, coshing and what else?"

The man who called himself O'Flynn licked his lips. There was a moment's pause. Perhaps because Dawlish's expression appeared to relax, a little confidence crept back into O'Flynn's manner."

"*You* can talk," he said, and it was almost a sneer.

Dawlish lit a cigarette, and studied his prisoner carefully. His rage had gone. He was beginning to understand what had made O'Flynn seem so confident of himself. He began to smile, faintly, as if he were amused; and it was hardly the little prisoner's fault that he did not know that, like that, Dawlish was in fact more dangerous than when he looked deadly.

"And why can I talk?" Dawlish asked, softly.

"Why, you ruddy hypocrite, putting on airs and living like a damned toff while all the time you're as bad as the worst of us!"

"How?"

"Come orf it," O'Flynn said, and again he was deceived by Dawlish's smooth manner. "Think I don't keep my ears close to the ground? You and your kind, you make me sick. You never take any risks, you leave that to me and the other Billy Mugginses, but you get the dough. Why—"

"So you really think I'm a fence," murmured Dawlish.

"Think? I *know*."

"Who told you?"

"What's up with you, you crazy?" asked O'Flynn, and he appeared to have been completely startled out of his fears. "It's often on the grapevine."

"Oh, is it?" said Dawlish, softly, and moved towards O'Flynn, taking his gun out. O'Flynn's eyes glinted with a swift return of fear, and he reared up against the wall. Clearly, he didn't understand; clearly, he had cause to be afraid.

"No, don't. Get away, don't—"

"Now you know what it's like to be scared out of your wits, too," Dawlish said, as if rejoicing. He moved fast, turned the gun in his hand and cracked it against the little man's temple. O'Flynn yelped. One blow was enough to put him out and to send him sliding down the wall. He lay on the floor in a crumpled heap, a threat to no man.

Dawlish went to the door, and called:

"Spare a minute, Alice, will you?"

She came from the kitchen; the fact that she had stayed there, and not peered through the keyhole of the study, was a remarkable tribute to her native honesty.

"Y-yes, sir?"

"Telephone Mr. Septimus, at the shop, and ask him to meet me at the back door in about half an hour's time," Dawlish said.

"Oo, I will, sir," said Alice, "I'll do it at once, sir. Mr. Septimus, at *Gale's*. I won't be a tick, sir."

She vanished as Dawlish grinned after her.

*   *   *

Dawlish was, he knew, taking a chance with Septimus Lee, the manager of *Gale's.* Maurice Gale had assured him that come joys or disaster, Septimus was wholly reliable. The two men, Gale and Dawlish, had first met when Gale was having trouble with a crooked customer but did not want the police involved. Dawlish had been able to help. Afterwards, Gale had taken on Septimus, an ex-lawyer, who had once worked for a Private Inquiry Agency after leaving his law practice under a cloud. So all that Dawlish officially knew of Septimus was good, but he did not know him well enough to be sure that he could trust him. Yet trust him he must, if he were to work without being in constant touch with the police.

Would Lee be prepared to take risks? Under the first shock of hearing what Dawlish wanted, he would probably reveal his true feelings.

Dawlish would soon know.

Gale's was a large shop in Gill Street, a small, exclusive street, and bombing had conveniently opened a way to its back door. The loading and unloading of large crate pieces for stock took place at that door. *Gale's,* as a curio and antique shop, attracted customers from all over the world. At one time it had been old-fashioned, gloomy, almost sinister; a connoisseur's joy. One had needed archaeological tools and qualifications to prise a way through the treasures hidden under years of dust. Maurice Gale had changed all that. Maurice was an up-and-coming young man who believed that the customer wanted to see what he was buying. He went all out to attract customers, and carried low-priced goods as well as single *objets d'art* which cost a fortune. He had spared nothing to dress the shop up well.

Now he was travelling the world, hunting for treasures, and Septimus Lee had a position of greater authority.

Septimus was a man of less than medium height, well-knit, well-built, handsome in a careless way; somewhere in the forties, Dawlish imagined. He had an air with him. He had something else which Maurice Gale might or might not know about; he had that indefinable 'something' which a man acquires when he has spent some time in jail.

Septimus was undoubtedly an old lag.

Trivett had found the Kroo emeralds at *Gale's*, but taken no action against Lee.

Yet Septimus Lee might be the culprit.

Dawlish knew that well, yet took a chance; he had to, if he were to work independently of the police.

Septimus Lee had a thin face with sharp features and heavily-lidded eyes—dark eyes in a fair-skinned face, a curious contrast.

He watched Dawlish drive up in the Humber, and moved forward to open the door. In the back of the car he saw a large Jacobean coffer, part of the furnishing of the St. John's Wood flat.

"Hallo, Sep," said Dawlish amiably. "Help me in with this."

"Good afternoon, sir. You didn't like it after all?"

"I wouldn't say that," said Dawlish, and grinned.

Septimus looked at him intently, thoughtfully.

Together, they took the coffer into the back of the shop. Here, it was almost dark, for no lights were on. They carried it up the narrow stairs, where Dawlish had to duck so as to save his head from the hanging rafters. This part of the premises had not been modernized. Nor had the storeroom, which was large, dusty and almost empty.

Another assistant came hurrying up from the shop.

"*I'll* do that, sir!"

"Thanks, I've managed," Dawlish said, and smiled at Septimus Lee. "Can they carry on for themselves downstairs, Sep?"

"I'll know the reason why if they can't," Sep said.

"Oh, we can manage," said the assistant eagerly.

"Thanks. Do." Dawlish smiled and watched him go. The door closed.

Septimus Lee was watching Dawlish with that thoughtful old-fashioned look; a wary look; the kind of look that a man might give to a policeman if he thought that the policeman was coming to arrest him. Or was that imagination? Those dark eyes in that pale face were startling. Spanish eyes in a Saxon face.

Septimus was still waiting.

Dawlish lit a cigarette and looked at him intently, wondering how best to try the man out.

He found the words he thought would do.

"Get that lid up, Sep, the chap ought to breathe," he said.

Septimus Lee went quite still for a moment, but his expression didn't change. Then he began to unlock the lid of the coffer. A good, steady nerve.

Dawlish went to a small room on the top floor, which had a dormer window, and from which he could see into Gill Street.

No one appeared to be interested in *Gale's*.

Dawlish went back to the storeroom. A few pictures stood round the walls, one or two oddments of furniture stood about, and a filing cabinet was in one corner; that was all.

Septimus was looking down into the terrified eyes of the man who called himself O'Flynn. He had come round while encoffined, and probably he had been more frightened in the past half hour than ever in his life before.

Dawlish joined Septimus, who had not turned a hair.

"Sep," he said, "this chap nearly killed an acquaintance of mine this afternoon, and he knows a lot that we ought to hear about. So we needn't be gentle with him." Again he gave the smile which had almost frozen the blood in O'Flynn's veins, and the man's lips actually formed an '*Oh!*' "And this is a sound-proof room, so it doesn't matter how much noise he makes," Dawlish went on in the same casual voice. "We haven't a lot of time, but I think he'll talk to us rather than the police."

Sep Lee's voice was as gentle as a dove's.

"I could heat an iron, sir, or boil a kettle. Heat treatment is usually—"

"No!" gasped O'Flynn, "no! I'll tell you all I know, I'll tell you!"

"Go on," Dawlish invited, and was delighted with Sep Lee's attitude.

O'Flynn began to talk. . . .

What Dawlish learned was not good.

For months past, his name had been bandied about in the East End of London, especially in those purlieus where criminals forgathered, whatever their particular line of business. He had become known as a buyer, a 'safe' buyer, of stolen jewels especially—although he was 'in the market' for anything that was easily negotiable.

One or two people had seen him, and talked about it; and the description was always the same.

He did his trading through third parties—and as far as O'Flynn knew and rumour had it, usually the same man or *woman*.

He paid a price that was neither mean nor generous, and in cash—always in small notes which could not be traced by the police. For a long time no one had known who he was. But in the past few months his name had been used frequently— always the same.

Dawlish, of *Gale's*.

O'Flynn had never seen him face to face, by night, or whenever they had business together; but he had made a point of seeing Dawlish enter and leave *Gale's,* as well as at the flat. He was quite sure that Dawlish was the buyer of stolen goods. It did not appear to have entered his head that he could be wrong; that showed clearly through the story he told and in the way he told it.

He said that his own speciality was a look-out man, ready to use a cosh so as to help make sure that anyone he was 'watching' for could escape trouble. Obviously he had no scruples, no pity and only one fear—of being found out.

He would do a 'job' for anyone who offered, and he had been given the job of breaking into the Litton Hotel and searching Fernandez's room and luggage. He had to find a photograph, of a girl and a man together.

"Did you find it?" asked Dawlish abruptly.

"It—it's in me pocket," O'Flynn muttered, and hurriedly put a hand to his pocket. So far, Dawlish had searched him for guns, but nothing else. He took out a photograph which must have been just the right size to fit into the pocket. "That—that's it."

There was the girl, Mepita.

There was also a man, standing by her side, who might easily be mistaken for Dawlish.

CHAPTER X

REPUTATION . . .

O'Flynn was in the storeroom, tied to a chair.

Dawlish and Septimus Lee were in the nearby office, at the head of the stairs. There was a long window, so placed that they could see into the main part of the shop below, but no one down there could see them. The office was furnished in modern fashion and there were many photographs of Maurice Gale, a handsome young man, and his wife; they had taken all the photographs between them.

Dawlish sat and Sep Lee stood.

"Sep," said Dawlish, offering cigarettes, "I think the time has come, as the walrus said, to have a little chat. You know O'Flynn's story. A lot of odd things have happened, all part of the same tale. I was almost left to rot in jail this morning, the frame-up was so clever that Bill Trivett was fooled into thinking I was handling stolen stuff. Know Trivett?" he asked almost abruptly.

Septimus gave a slow, dry smile.

"In a manner of speaking, sir, yes. He was in charge of the investigations which led *me* to rot in jail."

"You were rot-proof, apparently," Dawlish said dryly.

"I learned quite enough to persuade myself that I didn't want to go back," said Septimus Lee, "and I was lucky to find Mr. Gale willing to overlook my dereliction." He had a neat choice of word and a smile that was attractive. "He knew, of course, that I had served a seven years' sentence for embezzlement."

"Guilty?"

"Yes," said Septimus Lee frankly. "I was a solicitor, and I lost my head over a woman." He shrugged. "She might have been worth twelve months, but not seven years! She's now married with three children and a nine-to-six husband, and would probably deny we had ever known each other. May I volunteer a statement, Mr. Dawlish?"

"Yes. Thanks."

"Mr. Trivett was here this morning—I telephoned you several times to report, but you were out. I know nothing of this affair. I am not handling stolen goods. I am ready to co-operate in any way, although the police may be suspicious of anything I do. I have been aware of a greater interest than usual among several men from the Yard, but that happens periodically."

He stopped.

Dawlish smiled faintly.

"Sep," he said, "I think we're going to get along. But face it, there's a risk for us both but it's greater for you. If you slip up, the police will hold the past against you. Back out, if you'd rather."

"I think, everything considered, that I will stay in," said Septimus Lee. "After all, the good name of *Gale's* is at stake, and I would like to keep it clear. Also"—he smiled in much the same way as Dawlish had—"I'd enjoy seeing you work."

Dawlish grinned. "A deal, then. Good! Have you friends in the East End?"

"Enough," Septimus Lee said.

"That's fine. Check the story as far as you can, will you? Try to get a description of this woman who is supposed to act for me—and of the man as well." He glanced down at the photograph, and smiled faintly: "Do you think anyone would hang me for being like him?"

"There is a marked likeness," said Septimus, taking the question seriously. "I'll go at once, sir."

"Thanks," said Dawlish.

The manager went out, to call upon his contacts in the East End of London and to find how far O'Flynn's story was true.

Could he be trusted?

Dawlish could hope. . . .

He did not doubt the truth of O'Flynn's story; many details might be wrong but in the main it was probably accurate. He, Dawlish, had been living without the slightest idea that the plot was being built up. So had Sep Lee, if he had told the truth.

He liked Lee; would find it easy to trust him. But he couldn't do so completely. If only Tim Jeremy or Ted Beresford were here. . . .

Well, they weren't.

Dawlish stopped his wishful thinking, and thought of the one really helpful statement O'Flynn had made.

The prisoner had sworn that his instructions to get the photograph from Fernandez's room had come by telephone, that a woman had given him the order, that he was to meet her at nine o'clock that night, at a public house called the Red Bull. This was in a side street just off the Mile End Road.

There was plenty of time to meet her; and Dawlish was looking forward to it.

And one thing was leading to another.

Dawlish telephoned the *Daily Record* again, but without result. Allison hadn't reported since the morning, when he had left to meet Mr. Patrick Dawlish. . . .

"Thanks very much," said Dawlish politely.

He rang off.

Mepita had vanished, Fernandez had vanished, and now Allison. . . .

He rang the Yard.

Trivett wasn't in, but Sergeant Popple told him that they had not yet traced Fernandez, who had not returned to the hotel. His luggage was still there.

It was almost a case of vanishing people.

Dawlish seemed to know the girl who he had never met. The eyes and the face of her photograph haunted him. That wasn't his only worry. Fernandez had probably asked for anything he got, but Allison's disappearance was an anxiety. The reporter should have had a chance of sending a message by now.

He remembered seeing Allison walking in the wake of the man with the thick-lensed glasses, with the sun shining on his dark hair, and his shoulders square, his walk sprightly.

Where was he?

Earlier that day, Allison, who knew a great deal about Patrick Dawlish and held a much higher opinion of him than he did of most people, had walked briskly after the man with the down-at-heel shoes and the thick-lensed glasses.

Allison was smiling. Dawlish always knew exactly what he was doing, and would not make elementary mistakes; Dawlish had seen the man in front last night, and had a good reason for wanting him followed. Allison, with a nose for news, could see a big story breaking, although so far he had only the faintest glimmering of what it was.

The man stopped at a bus stop, and waited.

Allison went past, hailed a taxi, got in, and saw his quarry board a bus. The taxi-driver was obliging, and followed the bus, keeping close enough for Allison to watch everyone who got off.

The man with the thick-lensed glasses left the bus at a junction and turned along a side street of little houses. Allison paid off his cab, and followed the man, who turned into an ordinary little house, Number 29. Allison passed this, to make sure of the number, and then turned towards the corner, wondering whether to wait and see what happened here, or to go back to Dawlish. He was in no mood to venture much on his own; he wanted to know more about the case before he became a hero.

He decided to watch for half an hour, then telephone Dawlish's flat and keep telephoning until Dawlish answered. It wasn't very satisfactory; it seldom was when Dawlish left anyone else to follow a trail; Dawlish seemed to have a nose for the one which went in the right direction for results. But with the comforting certainty of a big story waiting, Allison did not complain.

It was pleasantly warm.

Two or three people walked along the street, and passed Allison.

No one approached Number 29, and for a while, no one came out of it. Then a man appeared—youngish, smart, well-set-up, fair-haired, startlingly like Dawlish. He wore different clothes, and it wasn't Dawlish, but at first sight the likeness was uncanny.

The man glanced swiftly at Allison, and then away.

Next, Allison heard a car.

He turned, and saw an open two-seater, with the hood right back, pulling alongside the man who had come from Number 29, Billitter Street. It was a bright, fresh green, and looked new. The girl at the wheel was in a bright, fresh green suit, and looked— refreshing. She wasn't exactly a chicken, Allison decided, but she was certainly something. Beautifully made up, hatless, with her hair groomed by a genius; and she had magnificent blue eyes. She glanced at Allison and then at the man.

Allison saw the man's frown, and realized that the girl understood that he was sending her a message. Her smile disappeared. She didn't look at Allison again, but the reporter saw that she had quite a figure. The car stopped, and she opened the door and got out, long legs sheathed in nylon; long, lovely legs.

The young man walked past.

He and the girl knew each other, but the man did not want it to be made clear to Allison.

The girl went to Number 29, rang the bell, and was admitted at once. Allison did not see who opened the door. He watched the man, who had now reached the end of the street. He felt a strange excitement, making his heart thud. He was on to something, this time Dawlish had chosen the wrong trail. The girl, Dawlish's double, the other man with the thick-lensed glasses, were all in the conspiracy, but—the young man had seen him and been wary.

The thing now was to get away, inform Dawlish, record descriptions of the people. Excitements built themselves up in Allison's mind. He did not go in the same direction as the tall young man who might have been taken for Dawlish but the other way.

He reached the corner.

A small man waiting round it stepped close to his side, jabbed something hard into his ribs, and said:

"Don't run, don't shout, just come with me."

He let Allison see the 'something': an automatic pistol.

The hold-up had come with devastating suddenness, and Allison knew that he hadn't a chance. This wasn't just bad; it could be deadly. His chief hope was that Dawlish or the police knew who they were fighting.

Did they?

* * *

Dawlish sat at the telephone in his study, listening to Septimus Lee. Felicity, her hat still on, gloves on a chair and looking serenely lovely in a dark brown suit and a white blouse, watched Dawlish intently. She knew he was feeling the strain; he was too remote from the affair, couldn't really close with it.

He said: "Right, Sep, thanks. . . . Yes, we'll meet at the Red Bull. . . . Oh, let him stay at the shop. . . . Good-bye." He rang off, and looked at Felicity, his head a little on one side. She didn't speak, but her eyes asked the questions.

"Lovelier than ever," he told her. "I could never be unfaithful, my darling!"

"Pat, what's happening now?"

"And so cold-blooded, too," mourned Dawlish. "'Tis not I who have changed, it is thee, beloved. Allison's missing. Fernandez is missing. Mepita is missing. A man who appears to be a friend of Fernandez, especially of Mepita, is in hospital with a cracked skull and a cut throat, and it's touch and go whether he'll live or die."

Felicity said, "Oh," and went and sat down abruptly.

"The man who attacked him is a prisoner at the shop," Dawlish went on, without turning a hair, "and he was persuaded to talk without us having to resort to the use of boiling oil. The plot has thickened! Sep Lee is one of us, I hope and trust."

"Pat," Felicity said very slowly, "that's enough fooling. I want to know everything."

"I'm telling you everything," Dawlish said earnestly. "Whilst you and I, Trivett, Sep Lee, and most of the upper world have been sitting pretty here, I've been nicely impersonated in London. I have won myself a big reputation as a reliable fence. I work through a tall young man and a beautiful woman, who is blonde with blue eyes, and has a figure that would turn most men's eyes the wrong direction. She is dubbed, with that unfailing resourcefulness of the Cockney, as the Blonde Doll. According to Sep, who has been doing a bit of research work, I've bought about two hundred thousand pounds' worth of sparklers and what not in the past six months, and from time to time someone has put a name on me. By planting the Kroo emeralds, the someone wanted me inside, out of the way. I'd like to know why. Quite an impressive case of mistaken identity," he went on, and grinned expansively—but he couldn't hide all his fears. "That, I think, is everything. Except that I've told Trivett something of this, and he's busy checking it. Mepita I don't know, so oughtn't to feel too worried about her, but Allison—"

"All this, and we've known nothing about it!" Felicity exclaimed in utter bewilderment.

Dawlish got up, and poured her a generous gin and Italian.

"Pooh, that's nothing. I was running around Europe with a dark-eyed señorita, and you didn't know a thing about it."

"That's not funny any longer."

"No, dear."

"What are you going to do?"

"Two things," said Dawlish. "It's nearly seven, and I'm going to wait until eight. If Allison hasn't turned up by then, I'm going to tell Trivett that he's missing. And at nine o'clock I'm going to see what the Blonde Doll looks like, she's due at . . ."

He explained.

Felicity did not utter a word of protest, which was so remarkable that it was almost miraculous.

"I don't know a thing more than that," Dawlish assured Trivett, on the telephone. "Allison went to follow the chap, and hasn't turned up. His newspaper hasn't heard a word from him. I'm worried, the *Record*'s worried, and I think he ought to go on record as missing."

"He's old enough to look after himself," Trivett growled, "we've enough to do without chasing after newspapermen who won't stick to their own business. But all right, I'll look round for him. Anything else?"

"I'm staggered at the amount of business I've done in the East End lately," Dawlish said brightly. "I must be about the biggest fence in London. No, Bill! Anything on Fernandez yet? Or the Spanish girl?"

"No."

"How about the injured chap—Corez?"

"He might pull through," Trivett said.

When he rang off, Dawlish rubbed the bridge of his broken nose, then confided in Felicity that he did not like the situation, particularly because Trivett hadn't warned him to be careful. Trivett undoubtedly guessed that he would play a lone hand, and would have him watched.

"But I'd rather make up here," Dawlish said, "it's much more comfortable."

Felicity echoed, "Make up?" in a resigned voice.

"My sweet, I can't go to the Red Bull and Blondie as I am," protested Dawlish, "I must go as a stranger." He chuckled, feeling the flush of excitement which he knew that Felicity hated at heart—but in this case, she could so easily understand. "I'm going to fall back on the simple thing, disguise." He hissed the word. "And if Trivett's watching the flat, I'll have to slip his man later. Meanwhile, I'm hungry. Think Alice is anywhere near ready with a meal?"

Alice was ready. . . .

Immediately after dinner, Dawlish went into the bedroom. Felicity was with him.

Felicity had brought a make-up box from the bedroom, opened it, and put it on the dressing-table; she got a towel and some other oddments for him. Now and again, as he worked on his face, he glanced at her in the mirror.

Dawlish changed in front of her eyes; her husband was no longer her husband. His skin, complexion, eyes, the shape of his nose, of his mouth and cheeks and forehead, all changed; even the bone formation seemed to change under the skilful influence of shading.

An older, tougher, darker man looked at her from the mirror.

Finished, he put on an old suit which had a padded back which took away a little from his height. Next he slipped some tools in a capacious inside pocket, finally put the automatic pistol into another pocket, with a spare clip of ammunition.

He patted this briskly.

Felicity said, "Must you take that?" although the words were only rhetorical.

"I'll be astonished if I have to use it," Dawlish said. "Don't worry, my sweet. I'd much prefer to break their necks!" He slipped into a huge raincoat. "Now I've to dodge that copper outside. That's if there is a copper. And you take the Austin to the Red Bull and leave it handy, will you? Then come back. I've a key for the Austin," he added.

"All right," Felicity said.

There was someone; he could see the man from the window. Trivett might simply be having the flat watched, which would imply that he—or his superiors—was not convinced that Dawlish was free from suspicion. Who could blame anyone for that in view of the reputation which had been won for him?

Dawlish—'the biggest fence in London'.

Dawlish, of *Gale's*; a byword among thieves and fences, mobsmen and coshboys.

The known facts spelt danger which could come from two directions. It could come from the police in their search for 'evidence', and from the unknown man who had assumed his name and was busy wrecking his reputation. Trivett would find the evidence so unbelievable that he would first reject it, would only slowly accept the possibility that it was true. But Trivett had to work on evidence.

Facts remained facts. He, Patrick Dawlish, had been impersonated for a long time. One matter arising was becoming obvious, although he hadn't pointed it out to Felicity. She probably knew, there wasn't much that she missed.

It was simple and it was menacing.

The moment Dawlish had learned of the impersonation, obviously the masquerader's days were numbered. He would probably try to make a final clean-up, and then vanish. To make himself secure, he would want the police, and the world at large, to find 'proof' that the crook was in fact Dawlish.

There lay the greatest danger; whatever 'proof' that the unknown would try to leave behind.

Dawlish entered the street and, keeping his raincoat collar turned up, walked briskly towards the end of Withy Street. His Humber was still outside. The Yard man might have instructions simply to watch the flat; if so, there was nothing to worry about. He might be here to follow anyone—and he might not be a Yard man.

Dawlish reached the corner.

The watcher followed him.

CHAPTER XI

THE BLONDE DOLL

Dawlish walked briskly along Marylebone Road, that main thoroughfare which ran through St. John's Wood and led to one of the main arteries out of London—and he was still followed. The man walked briskly, but shuffled a little. It might be Trivett's man—or it might be a friend, so to speak, of O'Flynn.

Dawlish boarded a bus.

The other man ran to catch up with it, succeeded, and jumped aboard. Dawlish, already on the top deck, looked down—and saw the man with the thick-lensed glasses.

This was the first really close look he had had at the man, who was younger than he had thought, pale-faced, with very fair cropped hair.

This man went inside the bus.

Dawlish stayed on top until they turned into the Edgware Road. Then he went down the narrow steps. As the bus stopped near Marble Arch, he jumped off. The man with the thick-lensed glasses followed him, very nimble of foot.

Crowds thronged Oxford Street. Neon lighting flashed a dozen colours, it was almost as bright as it would be at midday.

As if completely unaware that he had been followed, Dawlish took another bus, and got off at Victoria. He walked towards the station briskly, but without making it difficult for the other to keep up with him.

He approached the main line station.

Several taxis were waiting, but no queue of people. Making no attempt to hurry, Dawlish now sauntered past the taxis, as if waiting for someone. Two people took the first cab, soon the second and third were taken; only one was left. He moved towards it swiftly, opened the door and climbed in.

"Leicester Square!" he said clearly, and slammed the door.

The man with the thick-lensed glasses stared at him, looking almost malignant. But there was no other taxi in sight. This one swerved, and threw Dawlish against the corner. He looked out of the window, and saw his trailer staring after him.

He grinned to himself.

He changed taxis at Leicester Square, which was as bustling and crowded as Victoria, and took a second one as far as Aldgate. Next he took a bus along the wide and murky Mile End Road, getting off near the turning which led to the Red Bull. He was now sure that he had not been followed from Victoria and that it would be almost impossible to trace him.

He walked towards the public house, reaching the green painted door at five minutes to nine. The Austin was fifty yards along the street.

Would the Blonde Doll come in person?

The Red Bull was just another East End pub; from outside, the lighted windows had been inviting, beer advertisements showed up plainly. Outside, too, a man played a harmonica drearily, and didn't stop when Dawlish opened the door.

Hot, beer-laden air smote him; and there was a strong smell

of tobacco. The saloon bar was crowded. Dockers, dressed as if for work, with their heavy clothes and chokers, were by the bar. One or two smartly dressed men, with wasp waists and padded shoulders, were at one end. Two women and two men sat at the small tables near the windows. The hum of conversation didn't cease when Dawlish entered, although most of those present knew that someone else had come in.

By the bar, talking to a heavy-looking man whom he doubtless knew well, was Septimus Lee. But Lee's hair was fair, from bleach, and smoothed down with grease. His cheeks were sunken—an effect gained simply by taking out his dentures. His complexion made the big difference, though. He had darkened his skin, and his dark eyes no longer looked odd.

He glanced at Dawlish, but made no sign that he recognized him. That was a tribute to the disguise.

The clock, five minutes fast to give the landlord time to clear the bar at closing time, said nine-four. So it was one minute to nine—when the Blonde Doll, according to O'Flynn, was due to come and meet him.

A minute passed, while Dawlish ordered a pint of mild in a voice that grated, and which no one who knew him would have recognized. He took it to a table, and sat down so that he could watch the door.

Five minutes passed, and the woman didn't arrive.

He began to think of what he would do to O'Flynn.

Then the doors swung open, and a woman came in.

She wasn't exactly the type he had expected. She wore a bright yellow scarf round her head, and a few blonde curls poked from beneath it. Her eyes were heavily mascaraed, her eyelashes were false, her lipstick might have been laid on with a palette brush. She walked with a swaggering movement towards the bar, followed by a man dressed in a navy blue suit, wearing a collar and tie, and carrying a bowler hat. He was wiping his damp forehead.

"Wot'll you 'ave, ducks—port, as usual?"

"Okay, Charlie boy, port it is."

"Nice glass o' port," said Charlie boy, "and a pint of the usual for me." He went across to the bar.

It was nicely done, but for anyone on the look-out for it, unmistakable. The woman and the man looked round quickly, expecting to see someone who wasn't there. Their eyes met in disappointment. The landlord served Charlie boy, and he took the drinks to a table. They sat so that they could watch the door.

Sep said something to his companion, drank up his beer, and went out.

Dawlish stayed where he was.

The man and the woman also stayed for under an hour, showing increasing restlessness which they obviously tried to hide. The man smoked several cigarettes, the woman only one. Something in her pose more than her manner told Dawlish that she could be quite something to look at.

They said very little.

Just before ten, they left.

Dawlish followed, a few seconds afterwards.

The couple were already near the end of the street, visible in the light from a gas-lamp. Lee was on the other side of the road.

Dawlish quickened his pace. The couple turned the corner. A small car was parked there, and the woman went to it. Dawlish heard her say:

"You find out what happened to him, Charlie." Her voice was quite different from what it had been in the pub, lacked the loud, Cockney tone, and was easy and cultured. "I'll go straight back."

"Okay, Liz," the man said. "I can't understand what happened, though. The police didn't get him."

"Sure?"

"Oh, I'd know if he'd been pinched."

"If he's holding out—" the woman began, and then stopped, as if she knew that speculation was simply a waste of time. "Telephone me when there's any news, Charlie."

"I'll do that. 'Night."

"Good night."

The woman got into the small car, a dark saloon, and drove off. Dawlish waited until she was some distance along the road, and then went to the Austin. He drove off after her. Sep was watching the man with the bowler hat, and would deal with him if necessary.

Dawlish hoped.

The woman turned into the Mile End Road, and then went through the Aldgate district, next the deserted City with its ghostly tall buildings and narrow streets; then Fleet Street, the Strand and, eventually, Oxford Street. Twenty-five minutes later the car pulled up outside the small house where Allison had followed the man with the thick-lensed glasses.

She let herself in with a key.

Dawlish left the Austin round a corner, and waited for ten minutes. A man came out, and drove off in the woman's car. Dawlish still waited. Ten minutes later, the same man returned; probably he had been to garage the saloon car. He also let himself in with a key.

The street was very quiet. There was a little traffic in the main road at the end, but the sounds hardly came this far. Dawlish waited in the shadows, until he heard the heavy footsteps of a policeman on beat duty coming along. He stood in a shadowy doorway, watching the man, who passed without shining a light on him.

The man turned a corner.

A clock, not far off, struck eleven.

A light went on in the front window of Number 29; the shadow of a woman appeared against the curtains, but in a few seconds the light went out again.

Silence settled.

At half-past eleven, Dawlish moved towards the closed door. He examined the lock, an ordinary Yale, in the light from a street lamp. He was clearly visible to anyone who passed, but no one came into the street.

He opened his knife to a blade specially made to force Yale locks, which would have brought an angry scowl to Trivett's face. Before using this, he pushed the door, but it did not budge. His heart began to beat faster as he took out a pencil torch, and shone it at the join between the door and the door-frame. He could not see any bolts; there was a flange which would make it difficult to get at them.

A cyclist turned into the street, light swaying up and down. Dawlish drew back into the doorway and waited until the man had passed. He'd hardly gone before a young couple came dawdling along, arms round each other. Dawlish kept quite still until they had gone.

Then he went to the window and examined the sides in the light of his torch.

The first thing he saw was the wire of a burglar alarm.

He switched the torch off. His heart was beating much more swiftly now. The street was so long, and bare, there were few hiding places. At a big house, he would have had the shelter of a friendly wall, or trees, or a hedge. Here, there was nothing. Anyone passing could see him, unless he stood in the shadows. The street lamp was too close for comfort. He might break it with a stone, but if the policeman came here again and noticed that it was out, it might start an alarm.

What about the back way?

He moved from the window towards the street, and as he did so, a car turned the corner. He moved swiftly to another doorway. Headlights flashed on for a moment, then went off. He wasn't sure whether he was seen. He stood tensely in a doorway several removed from Number 29. The car drew up, quite near him, and three men got out.

One was tall, youthful—difficult to see in the poor light, but probably his double.

One had thick-lensed glasses.

The third was O'Flynn.

So O'Flynn had escaped, or been released.

Dawlish watched the trio, as they waited for the door to be opened, then went in.

CHAPTER XII

THE LITTLE HOUSE

Dawlish waited for another five minutes before moving forward again. This time he used the cracksman's tool, turned the lock, and pushed. The door yielded. He opened it wide enough to step through. There was a light in the hall; light framing a door at the end of a passage alongside the stairs.

He closed the front door behind him.

He could hear radio music, coming from the downstairs room; that was all.

He went up the stairs, saw another door framed in light, and heard voices; but the door of this lighted room was solid. At first he could only catch an odd word or two. Then he realized that they were talking in Spanish.

He turned away from this door. There were two others on the landing, as well as a narrow passage which ended in a blank wall. He tried the handle of the first door, which opened into an empty bedroom. He closed it, tried the next—and found it locked.

His pick-lock blade slid into the lock. He twisted it. The lock went back very easily.

The room beyond was dark, but Dawlish heard a sound, as of someone stirring or turning over in bed. He closed the door. The sound was repeated, but that was all. He shone the pencil torch about the room—and the bright beam fell on to Allison's face, on to a bruise at his temple, on to bloodshot eyes and a gag tied tightly round his mouth.

Dawlish cut the cloth of the gag, and pushed pillows behind Allison's back. Allison tried to mouth words, but could only make a hoarse, whispering sound. There was a hand basin in the room. Dawlish poured a little water into a glass on the mirror shelf and took it to the newspaperman.

Allison swallowed, greedily.

His wounds weren't serious.

There was no other sound but his heavy breathing.

Dawlish opened the door and looked into the empty passage. He could still hear those murmuring voices. There was no noise from downstairs. He had to make sure that Allison could look after himself before he did anything else, but above everything, he wanted to hear what was being said; and to talk to the Blonde Doll.

Dawlish cut the cords at Allison's ankles, and massaged his wrists and ankles gently. The newspaperman kept mouthing. The gag had bitten tightly into the sides of his mouth, and the blood now circulating must be causing him agony, but he didn't show it.

At last, he managed to gasp: "Who—who are you?"

Dawlish spoke in his normal voice:

"Take it easy, Ally."

"Pat!" exclaimed Allison. "Why, I can't believe—"

"Shut up!"

Allison fell silent, but was still badly shaken. It was several seconds before he muttered:

"They're killers."

"As if I didn't know."

"Don't take any chances."

"Stop wasting your breath," Dawlish whispered. "Do you know where the girl is?"

"No, I—"

Allison stopped. There was a sound at the door, which Dawlish heard as well as the newspaperman. He stood up and moved across the room. The sound wasn't repeated. He watched the handle, expecting it to turn, but it didn't move. He listened, intently, and could hear nothing.

Had it been imagination?

He turned the handle gently and pulled. The door wouldn't open, it had been locked from the outside.

Dawlish had been seen to come in and was trapped; they were both prisoners now.

Like everything else in this affair, the move had come swiftly, without a moment's warning. And unless they could break out, this might be fatal.

Dawlish tried to make the pick-lock catch in the lock barrel, but the keyhole was blocked. He pulled desperately, exerting his great strength, but the door wouldn't budge.

Allison was staring at him.

Dawlish moved towards the window, stood to one side, and drew the curtain back. There were iron bars. Each discovery was worse than what had gone before. This was deadly. The night was filled with deep menace, greater than anything that had gone before, worse because it was wrapped in mystery.

Then he smelt burning.

The smell crept insidiously into the room. For the first few seconds he had not realized what it was, but suddenly he knew, beyond all doubt. In a sudden frenzy, he went back to the door and hurled himself against it. It hardly moved.

Allison croaked: "I can smell—fire."

"Someone has had a nasty idea," Dawlish said, and made himself speak lightly. He moved from the door to the window, pulled the curtain aside again, and saw the iron bars again, the thick, toughened glass beyond. Fear really took possession of him. He felt real panic.

There was no way out through the window.

He might be able to get the door down, given time. *Time.*

The smell of burning was much stronger. He thought he could see smoke. He found himself wondering how it was the fire had started so quickly, why he hadn't noticed it from the beginning.

Allison began to cough.

Dawlish took the toolbag from his pocket, opened it, and took out two small plastic phials. He was prepared for most emergencies, because there had been so many in the past. Living dangerously made one sharp-witted; and he knew what was likely to be needed. He held the phials steadily, knowing that Allison was watching every move he made. He put the little containers on the floor, then opened a cardboard tube, which looked like a large firework. He opened the end of this and poured a stream of brownish powder on to the floor and over the first two phials.

He struck a match.

Smoke from the door curled up about it.

He went down on one knee and put the match to the trail of gunpowder, then turned back to Allison. His heart hammered, and he could see the dread in Allison's eyes.

Allison had had a bad time already.

"Get down on the floor," Dawlish ordered. "We'll be all right."

He helped Allison off the bed, and to lie on the floor on his stomach. "Cover your ears with your hands," Dawlish added, and then lay down beside the journalist, pressing his hands against his ears, waiting for the blast.

The floor felt hot.

He found breathing difficult; was almost suffocated. He gritted his teeth, still waiting for the explosion. Was there something wrong with the powder? Was it damp? Was it too old? He had bought it years ago, and—

It roared!

He felt the blast first, then the explosion. He was lifted off the floor, thrown upon Allison so heavily that the breath was knocked out of his body. He went deaf. He imagined he could hear a roaring but it was only the blood in his ears. He could not move for what seemed a long time, although he was agonizingly conscious of a sense of urgency.

It was so hot. Stifling.

He felt as if he were burning.

He could hardly breathe.

Then he managed to struggle to his feet, and stand swaying. He saw Allison move. He bent down, and helped the newspaperman to his feet. They turned towards the door. A great hole had been blasted in that and in the wall, and flames leapt through it, into the room, flames were already licking at the furniture.

The one chance was that the landing would hold.

Dawlish reached the doorway first. He could see the flames on the stairs, licking their way downwards; the fire had started on the landing. He thought he saw a face, looming through the smoke. He put an arm round Allison's waist, and gritted his teeth as they went towards the landing. For a moment they trod on flames, and flames were about them as high as their shoulders. The smell of burning cloth came, strong, terrifying.

Dawlish felt a crackling sound as his hair singed.

Then they reached the stairs, almost fell down them, reached the front door, and heard people calling out, heard a loud knocking.

He must avoid being questioned by the police. He carried a burglar's outfit, jemmy, tools that could damn him; he dared not be identified as Dawlish, or the Yard men would have 'proof' that he had turned bad.

A constable, a short man in his shirt-sleeves and a small boy were in the doorway. The constable almost fell into the hall as the door opened. Dawlish let Allison go, caught up the last vestige of his strength, pushed past the trio, and ran into the street. There was a small crowd of startled people, but no one stopped him, and he reached the Austin.

The engine roared.

Superintendent William Trivett, in what must surely have been his best grey suit, looked at Felicity rather as a hawk might look at an impudent sparrow; although Felicity bore not the slightest resemblance to a sparrow. She was very calm, poised, hand-some, and patient.

"I'm sorry, Bill," she said, "but the doctor said don't wake him, and I'm not going to let you."

"Damn the doctor. He's as right as rain, and—"

"He's asleep," Felicity said solemnly. "He was out on his feet when he came home."

"Was he burned?"

"*Burned?*" echoed Felicity. "Gracious, no! And you can talk until you're blue in the face, but without a warrant you're not going to see him until he wakes up."

"You're worse than he is," grumbled Trivett. "You're sure he's not badly hurt?"

"Oh, yes," said Felicity. "A spare can of petrol caught fire in the garage." She had set it alight; the police could not prove a lie. "Do you know what else happened?"

"I can guess," Trivett growled. "He found Allison, and someone either tried to burn them alive, or they started a fire while getting out. Allison's in hospital, and likely to stay there for days." Trivett went on. "No, he hasn't named Pat as his rescuer. He came round, said that he was kidnapped, and that a stranger rescued him."

"Not the police?" marvelled Felicity.

"I always said that you were a darned sight worse than Pat himself," Trivett said, but there was an amused gleam in his eyes. "Did you know where he was going?"

"No," Felicity said with admirable conviction. "But when he comes round, I'm sure he'll tell you everything. Unless," she added sweetly, "you have found some little things out for yourself."

Trivett put his head on one side.

"If you start believing in his omniscience, the pair of you will end up in jail," he declared, and Felicity realized that he was really in earnest. "Listen, Fel. The story that Pat is buying stolen jewels—goods of all kinds—is as thick as fleas round the East End. No one's identified his photograph beyond all doubt but several think it's the right one. On circumstantial evidence, Pat wouldn't have a chance. You know that I don't think he'd be so crazy, but I'm not the law or Scotland Yard or even the Home Secretary. I have to find out facts, and these facts don't look good for Pat. I may believe in the impersonation, but it will soon be a case of putting Pat in dock to prove that he has been impersonated. Don't make any mistake. It's ugly."

"I won't," Felicity said, very quietly.

"Does he suspect Sep Lee?" Trivett asked abruptly.

"He's never said so."

"He'll be a fool to trust Sep far," Trivett said.

"Perhaps he will," agreed Felicity. "But, Bill . . ." she paused.

"Yes?"

"I'm pretty sure that he will handle it as well as you can."

Trivett grunted.

"Did you find any of the people who lived at the house that was burnt?" Felicity switched the subject.

Trivett told her what he knew, and what he thought it safe for Dawlish to know.

Felicity passed the story on to Dawlish, about three hours later. He was sitting up against the pillows, with a breakfast tray in front of him, although it was after twelve.

Felicity sat with her face towards the window.

The police had sent Allison to hospital.

The fire had been too fierce for the firemen to put it out until not only Number 29, but the houses on either side of it were gutted. There was no indication that anyone had been burned to death. Neighbours testified to hearing cars leave, shortly before the explosion—the explosion, not the fire, had roused the people.

The three houses, it was now known, had been turned into one. No one knew much about the people who lived there. Descriptions tallied with that of the Blonde Doll and a man very like Dawlish.

So far as Trivett was concerned, none of this was likely to be satisfactory.

He had learned that *Gale's* had been raided, but appeared to know nothing of O'Flynn, the little man who had been released.

The only other news was of Corez, who was nearly out of danger.

"I don't exactly feel like getting up and pushing a bus over,"

Dawlish said, although doing great justice to the bacon and eggs. "I don't know that we've got much further." He speared a piece of bacon. "Mepita might have been at the house, but that's only a guess. The bunch saw the danger and cleared out in a hurry. But Trivett still seems to think that I might be charged with buying and selling stolen goods."

"He said so," Felicity agreed.

"I don't like fighting shadows," said Dawlish quietly. "It looked as if it were going to work out nicely, and instead we're back where we started, without Fernandez, Mepita, the crooks or even Blondie." He sipped his coffee. "We've even lost our prisoner." He paused. "How did Sep Lee get on?"

"He telephoned to say that the man he followed got away," Felicity said. "Pat, do you trust Sep Lee?"

Dawlish said: "I want to. And if he's not trustworthy, we're really at our beam ends—except for a photograph of Mepita and the man who married her in the name of Patrick Dawlish, and Corez. You haven't let anyone get hold of that photograph, have you?" he added hastily.

"I put it in the safe," Felicity said.

"The true guardian angel," Dawlish praised; then brooded for a while.

Felicity stood up.

"If you're thinking what I'm thinking," she said, "you're worried because you and Allison actually saw this man and the women, which means you two can identify them. Possibly anyone else can. They've tried to kill you once and they've proved they don't mind employing murderers," Felicity went on. "Nice situation, darling, isn't it? Are you *sure* you wouldn't like to take a nice long holiday? Say a month in the South of France, or—"

"Spain," murmured Dawlish, and really startled her.

"You'll do no such thing!"

"Oh, I don't know," mused Dawlish. "Sunny Spain, where the oranges grow—"

"It's not the season for oranges."

"All right, oranges or almonds or what you like," said Dawlish. "I want a talk with Fernandez. I only know one place where I might find Fernandez. After all," he argued, "you could take a camera, you've never been to Spain. You ought to be urging me to do it instead of—"

"You haven't the slightest reason for thinking that he would go back to the Barcelona address he gave you on his card," Felicity said hotly. "It's just like you to get a crazy idea like this in your head. With any luck the doctor will make you stay in bed until you're sane."

She went to the door, made a face at him, and went out, closing the door sharply.

Nothing developed in the next three days. Trivett called three times, but couldn't break Dawlish's story. Allison had kept his secret. Sep Lee reported in person and in some detail. If he realized that he could be more readily suspected now, he showed no sign of anxiety.

The back way into the shop had been forced when O'Flynn had been released, but nothing had been taken.

On the morning of the fourth day, Allison telephoned from his flat in the Adelphi to say that he was about again, that even while at death's door his influence was being extended, and he could say for certain that Carlos de Ciento y Fernandez, a young man of aristocratic lineage, little money and great pride, had returned to his flat on the Avenida Republica, in Barcelona.

The *Record* knew now that Fernandez had a sister, but had not been able to trace her.

"If I were fit enough I'd get my old man to assign me

to Barcelona for a few weeks," Allison said, "but I can't persuade him that I'm well enough! Why don't you go, Pat? Things have quietened down here." He paused. "Temporarily," he added, and went on soberly: "But I have it on the highest authority that the police are going through every tittle of evidence to prove you're the Big Bad Fence, trying to cover your tracks with the impersonation story. Trivett's on your side, but the rest of the Yard are *anti*. There's a lot of evidence that could look black against you. I shouldn't just sit back and await events, if I were you."

"That's not my idea at all," Dawlish agreed. "But I'm going to see Señor Ramon Corez before anything else. Wouldn't you?"

As he spoke, there was a sound at the door. Felicity looked impatiently at it, knowing that Alice was out. Reluctantly she moved towards the door, saying:

"You're *not* going to Spain this year, next year, or—"

"Okay, Pat," Allison said into the telephone, and added: "Take care of yourself, they don't love you, you know." He paused. "I wonder if . . ."

"Yes?"

"Been hesitating about this for some time," Allison went on, "but I didn't know whether I ought to open my big mouth. I've decided that I should. Septimus Lee, who works at *Gale's*, once did—"

"Seven stretch," Dawlish said.

"Oh, lor'," groaned Allison, "what's the use of thinking anything's news to you? But seriously—be careful."

"Careful," said Dawlish earnestly, "is a weak and anaemic word for what I'm going to be. 'Bye."

He rang off, and looked up into Felicity's eyes, smiling in a beguiling fashion. The idea of going to Spain had come very suddenly. He liked the prospect very much. He could guess that

Felicity felt that they would be in far greater danger in a foreign land, and certainly it would be more difficult, since neither of them spoke the language. But as Fernandez was there . . .

Dawlish stopped smiling.

Felicity had a letter in her hand; a pretty thing, with a red and blue border, used by all nations but Great Britain and most of the Commonwealth to distinguish air mail letters from ordinary mail.

She looked stormy.

"This," she said, "is from Tim. You *hound*!"

"*Tim?*" Dawlish's heart leapt. Tim Jeremy was the very man he needed, and this might mean that he was on his way home. He grabbed. "Gimme!"

She held the letter up, away from him.

"I've a good mind," she declared, "to burn it before you can read it. You *beast*!"

"Hound, beast, savage or just plain human male, I want that letter," said Dawlish, and grabbed again. He got it. He looked at the postmark and the stamps. He gaped. "Why, it's from *Spain*!" he cried.

"As if you didn't know," Felicity shrilled.

CHAPTER XIII

MESSAGE FROM SPAIN

Dawlish opened the letter slowly; it was so securely stuck down that he would have torn it had he been careless. Felicity watched, and he hoped that she was beginning to realize that she was wrong; that he had not known that Tim Jeremy, blessed Tim Jeremy, was in Spain.

The postmark, in fact, was Barcelona.

Dawlish opened the letter at last. It was not a long one, and Tim's large, ham-fisted writing covered a great deal of space. He had written:

Hell, it's hot, and I mean hot. I do not like Bull Fighting. I do like Spanish señoritas. I am almost sorry I'm married. Joan, by the way, sends her love. It is because of my love for her that we are in Spain. I told her she was bound to lead to my undoing. She says is there anything you or Felicity wants and she doesn't mean nylons. Or that ridiculous perfume Fel likes simply because it's hard to get. She certainly doesn't mean a case of sherry. Steel is very steely out here. How about a nice chandelier? Seriously, we're doing nicely, thank you, in 90 or so in the shade. How Joan weathers it I don't know. She has met the friend of a school friend—you know what these girls are like—and so we're staying for another week. Under my protest, but you know how much that's worth. Love. Hell, it's hot—I'm attaching my seal, in sweat.

Tim.

Felicity was reading by Dawlish's side.

"So you didn't know," she conceded reluctantly.

"I didn't know, and Tim doesn't know what's coming to him, and Joan"—Dawlish grinned delightedly. "This will teach her to want to stay another week because she's met a girl-friend!" He hugged Felicity so tightly that she gasped. "Tim can get cracking and we needn't go to Spain. Yet!" He hugged Felicity again. "I wonder if they'll be at the hotel—the Toledo, isn't it?" He let Felicity go, picked up the paper then hurried to the telephone.

"Of course he'll be out," said Felicity tartly. "You waste time, you waste money . . ."

Dawlish put in the call, which apparently aroused no surprise at the telephone exchange, lit a cigarette, and waited hopefully. After a while, Felicity melted. In fact, Felicity showed the fear which had taken possession of her, as Dawlish knew well. Because of that, she was not really herself.

"If you *must* go to Spain," she said out of the blue, "you're not going alone."

"Didn't I invite you?" asked Dawlish. "Surely—"

The telephone rang, and he grabbed it; but the wild hope that the call to Spain had come through so quickly was promptly dashed. The voice was Sep Lee's. He did not want to suspect Sep Lee of having let O'Flynn out of the storeroom at *Gale's,* but the suspicion was there.

"Yes, Sep," he said.

"I think I've found a little evidence," Sep said, almost prosaically. "I've discovered where O'Flynn is living now, Mr. Dawlish.

It's a small house in the East End, not far from the Red Bull. Shall I deal with him alone, or would you rather handle it yourself?"

The question spoke volumes. Sep was really asking whether Dawlish trusted him, or whether he felt inclined to leave anything at all to a man who had served a stretch. There was no time to ponder, to weigh the pros and cons. Dawlish had to back his judgment as against his inclinations, and had to back it quickly.

"Check him yourself, Sep," he said. "We want the Blonde Doll and Charlie boy. O'Flynn himself doesn't matter much."

"I'll deal with him," said Septimus Lee.

He sounded pleased; voiced a kind of satisfaction which might really express what he felt. But there was a chance that he was playing a big bluff. He would want to create the impression that he was doing everything he could, and might be prepared to give O'Flynn away, even if the man were working in the same racket.

"Call me when you can," Dawlish said.

He rang off.

He knew from Felicity's expression that she doubted his wisdom; but there was nothing more to be done. She did not speak about it. They moved about the flat uneasily for the next hour, intent on the telephone. The case had got under their skin; and Dawlish knew that one of the worst aspects, for Felicity, was the fact that there was so much circumstantial evidence against him.

It didn't exactly cheer him up.

If he left for Spain, would it look as if he were going to run for cover?

Would he be allowed to leave the country, anyhow?

Was Mepita in England or in Spain? If it came to that, was she dead or alive?

Her brother had reached Barcelona . . .

The telephone rang.

Dawlish leapt towards it, and Felicity sped towards the extension like a ballet dancer in a passionate moment of renunciation. Dawlish dropped down on a convenient chair, and lifted the receiver.

"This is Patrick Dawlish," he announced.

"Oh, yes, Mr. Dawlish, your call to Barcelona is through. Mr. Jeremy is waiting."

"Bless your heart," Dawlish breathed.

"You're through, Barcelona," said the operator, with a note of faint reproof in her voice.

"*Tim*," boomed Dawlish.

"*Patrick Dawlish,* whoever would believe it?" boomed Tim Jeremy. "No—emphatically. I have no pesetas to spare if you should happen to come."

His voice was loud and clear; he might have been in London at the end of a threepenny dial call.

". . . sorry, old boy," Tim went on.

"Tim," Dawlish declared, "you're getting fat and lazy."

"Fat? I? Idiot. In fact, imbecile," Tim Jeremy went on, really warming up. "I resent—"

"You want some work," said Dawlish.

"I want *what*?" asked Tim, faintly. "I couldn't have heard aright."

But he had; there was a note in his voice which told Dawlish so. He knew that 'work' was a euphemism. He would be excited at the prospect of a particular kind of labour whenever and wherever it came. Dawlish could picture his face, very lean, leathery, probably dark brown from the Spanish sun; and his grey eyes eager for more punishment.

"Pencil handy?" asked Dawlish.

"Right here, m'lord."

"I'll spell the name," Dawlish said, and spelt Fernandez's name; then Mepita's and added: "Possibly calling herself Dawlish." Next he gave the address that he had, on the Avenida Republica. "For a start," Dawlish went on, "I just want to make sure whether one of them or both of them are in Barcelona. Don't take any chances, it's a bit nasty."

"And I a married man," Tim said. He chuckled. "You'd never believe! Joan is spending all her time with a girl-friend, some beauty treatment or other, this is just the thing the doctor ordered, I was getting whatever's the masculine for coquettish. I'll call you as soon as I've anything definite, Pat. Anything else?"

"No, I—"

"Pat!" called Felicity into the extension. "I mean, Tim!"

"Good lord!" exclaimed Tim Jeremy. "I could have sworn I heard the female voice malign. Don't tell me that she's tapping your line."

"Go and boil—" began Felicity, and then recovered and became much calmer; in fact, almost maliciously polite. "I'm so glad I was on the line, Tim, Pat isn't at all well. It's all affecting his head. I think, he isn't exactly certifiable but he certainly ought to see a psychiatrist. He forgot to tell you that he's being impersonated, and that what he really wants you to do is to find out if there's anyone who looks like him in Spain. I mean—"

"Oh, don't qualify it," said Tim Jeremy earnestly. "After all there are only thirty million people or so over here, and finding another Pat would be easy. Er—has Felicity scored a hit, Pat?"

"I don't know what I would do without her," Dawlish said sweetly. "Listen, Tim." He described the Blonde Doll exactly as Allison had described her; and also the young man with her. "That's about the lot—the Spanish brother and sister, this pair, and a man who looks more or less like me and might possibly be in Spain. Any one of them will be worth a fortune."

"Trust you to make a profit," Tim said. "All right, Sonny Jim, leave it all to Uncle Tim. 'Bye."

He rang off.

Dawlish put the receiver down, ran his finger down the curved line of his broken nose, then went towards the other telephone and, when he reached Felicity, pulled her towards him and gently kissed her forehead.

"A reward for that," he said, "remind me tonight!" His eyes gleamed. "Thanks, my sweet, I must be slipping."

"Slipping?" echoed Felicity. "You couldn't slip any further." Unexpectedly, he saw that she was in earnest. "I just can't bottle it up any longer," she went on, "I *can't*. You're crazy to trust Sep Lee. He almost certainly let O'Flynn out, and—"

"All right, my darling," Dawlish said. "He's on trial now."

But that did not satisfy her.

He spent the rest of the afternoon and evening at *Gale's*, putting the business affairs in order sufficiently to justify him leaving the country for a week or two, if need be. When he returned to the flat, Felicity guessed what he had been doing, but could find no enthusiasm. He did not blame her.

He entered their room and found her staring at the picture of Mepita Fernandez; and he could tell from her expression that she was still genuinely worried about the girl.

At half-past eight, the telephone bell rang.

Dawlish answered; and in a moment knew that trouble had come much nearer.

"Pat," said a man whom he knew well, "I want a chat with you, in secret. Meet me at Mile End Road Tube station in an hour's time, will you?"

Dawlish said very slowly: "Yes. Yes, Bill."

"Good," said Superintendent William Trivett of the Yard. "Don't be late."

There was no mistaking his voice, and he was a friend, remember. There had been a dourness in his voice which on its own was alarming; and when added to the circumstances, became almost sinister. Why should Trivett want a secret rendezvous? What could he want that he couldn't say in public; or at least when he met Dawlish openly?

It added greatly to the tension.

"If you're sure it was his voice," Felicity said, "I suppose you'll have to go."

"Oh, it was Bill."

Felicity looked at her watch. "Well, if you're to be at the Mile End Road on time, you'd better get going," she said. "It'll take you half an hour."

"I've ten minutes yet," protested Dawlish.

It meant dodging the police, who were watching outside; and he needed time for that. It meant moving fast through the London night. It meant a meeting with a Yard official who sounded as if he carried all the trouble in the world, and was getting ready to pass it on to Dawlish.

Nine minutes from the time he had spoken, Dawlish was ready. In nine and a half minutes he was actually half-way down the first flight of stairs, with Felicity watching him from the door; and then the telephone bell rang again. He saw her start. She didn't speak but turned to hurry towards the instrument, guessing that he would wait to find out who it was. He watched her shadow moving, and getting further away. His own shadow fell as far as the first landing. Nothing moved in the house except Felicity. He heard her speak, quietly but clearly.

"This is Mrs. Dawlish . . ."

"*Who? . . .*"

"Yes, I'll call him," she said, and Dawlish knew that she didn't like the caller, had no enthusiasm for him at all. Dawlish hurried back and met her in the doorway. "It's Septimus Lee," she announced. "He wants you to go and see him—and you can't do that *and* see Trivett. You'll be crazy if you let Trivett down."

CHAPTER XIV

SECRET WARNING

Dawlish picked up the receiver, conscious of Felicity's almost accusing glare; conscious, too, of his own increasing tension. Felicity was right, he mustn't let Trivett down, yet this call might be urgent.

"Yes, Sep?" Nothing in his voice indicated his uncertainty. "What's on?"

"Mr. Dawlish, I think we've got them." Septimus Lee couldn't keep the excitement out of his voice. "There's O'Flynn and the man named Charlie—remember him?—and a couple of others. The blonde woman isn't there and there's no one like you, but this mob's all together. I thought you'd want to know in a hurry. They . . ."

He paused.

"They're going to break up at a quarter past ten," Septimus Lee told him. "They're at a restaurant in Soho, the *Liquid Gold*. I know they'll break up at ten-fifteen, they've ordered a car for then. Will you be there?"

"On the dot, Sep," promised Dawlish. "Nice work. Thanks. So long."

He rang off.

He wasn't surprised at the way Felicity looked at him, and he didn't blame her. It wasn't a good case. He supposed that the way it had been thrust upon her had been more of a shock than either of them had realized; it had meant that they kept at cross-purposes nearly all the time.

"There's time to see both Bill and Sep," he said, and tried to be reassuring.

"If you trust Septimus Lee," Felicity said, "you'll deserve everything that happens to you."

Dawlish drove through the quiet of London's evening, going through side streets and then across to the Victoria Embankment, so as to avoid the West End and the traffic. For a while he had the sluggish Thames for company, and could see the reflected light dancing on its murmuring bosom. Occasionally he could see the lights in the sky on high buildings, and St. Paul's, floodlit, a massive, dominant landmark. He cut away from the river at Blackfriars and was soon passing the cathedral beneath the shadow of the huge dome. He wasn't thinking about St. Paul's; only about Bill Trivett, Sep Lee and Felicity. Why did Felicity feel so sure that Sep Lee could not be trusted? Feminine intuition? He knew better than to laugh such a thing away; he had known her right when all logic and his own powers of reasoning had convinced him that she was wrong.

He sped through the dark city.

London sprang to life again at Aldgate, where some street traders were still pushing their barrows, and there was light and life and bustle. He drove along the Mile End Road, infuriated by a lorry which stopped him from making speed, until he reached the tube station, brightly lighted outside, but gloomy where the steps led down towards the tunnels and the trains. He parked the car in a side street, and then made sure that he hadn't been followed. He reached the entrance to the station, and had seldom been more on edge or more wary. He had tried to convince himself that there was no chance that someone had imitated Trivett's voice, but why should he feel so sure? Trivett's voice was quite distinctive, and anyone who wanted him, Dawlish, at a particular rendezvous might well believe that the certain way to get him was to pretend that Trivett wanted him there.

He stepped inside the station.

A man stood alone just inside and close to the wall. Lamplight shone on his cloth cap and his choker; it was Trivett, dressed for an East End raid; dressed to make sure that no one could easily recognize him. Only a trick of the light and the fact that Dawlish knew him well made sure of quick recognition. Dawlish joined him.

"Playing hide-and-seek?" he asked.

Trivett didn't smile, and Trivett was looking grim. It was bad all right. He moved, offering cigarettes.

"Pat," he said, "I could be drummed out of the Force for this. But your head's very near a noose. Corez was murdered tonight."

Dawlish didn't speak.

He thought of the Spaniard whose life he had saved because he had arrived at the Litton Hotel at the crucial moment. Now Corez, friend of Fernandez, had been murdered, the whole evil business was going on and on.

"Got the killer?" he asked.

"We picked up two men who saw someone go into the nursing home." Trivett's voice was low-pitched, almost hoarse—as if something hurt him. "A big man, your build, fair-haired. Any witness will swear it was you." He paused; and when Dawlish didn't speak, he burst out savagely: "Why the hell did you go and see Corez without telling me?"

"Wrong," Dawlish said, softly.

"Don't be a damned fool! You were there, you were seen. Listen, Pat, *I* know you wouldn't kill, I know you're not in this racket, but I can't do any more about it. The evidence is piling up. Two or three men at the Yard have hinted pretty broadly that I'm not taking action because you and I are close friends. It wouldn't surprise me if I were taken off the case by morning. That's how bad it is."

Dawlish said: "I wasn't at the nursing home.'

"All right," growled Trivett. "Keep telling the big lie in the hope of being believed."

"No lie," Dawlish insisted. Trivett didn't speak; so Trivett wasn't convinced. Hour by hour, this got worse. "Bill," Dawlish went on at last, "what do you really know about Septimus Lee?"

"He spent seven years in jail for embezzlement. I've never heard anything else against him. Your friend Maurice Gale knew. For the past few days he's been ferreting about in the East End. Your orders?"

"Yes."

"It's a waste of time. Listen," Trivett went on savagely. "There is evidence that you were seen at the scene of the murder of Corez about half an hour before he was found dead. Do I have to say anything else?"

"No," said Dawlish, very quietly. "No. Thanks, Bill."

"If you're at your flat tomorrow morning," Trivett said, "you'll probably be picked up. You'd better have a good story ready." He flicked his cigarette away, and it curved a red arc to the ground. He turned away from Dawlish, trod on the glowing tip and put it out, as if he were extinguishing a life. A man who was hanged by the neck until he was dead would die as quickly as that.

Trivett disappeared.

Dawlish lit a cigarette for himself, and moved away from the station. Trivett had already lost himself in the crowd. Trivett had proved himself a friend all right; and because of his friendship, was in danger of being thought unsound, disloyal to the Yard.

Crazy?

What Trivett had said was simple: that Dawlish would be wanted for murder next morning, that no one was likely to believe him when he said that he hadn't been to the nursing home where Corez had been murdered. "Disappear," Trivett had said, in effect, "or you'll find yourself in jail. If you want to work this job out for yourself, keep away from your flat. You're on the run."

No one could have made it clearer.

With anyone but Trivett, Dawlish might have believed that it was a ruse to get him to run, and so strengthen the impression of guilt. Trivett wouldn't play the game that way: Trivett was wholly serious.

It was a quarter to ten. They hadn't taken long. There was comfortable time to get to the *Liquid Gold,* a little restaurant in Soho with a big name for its cellar.

Dawlish went to the Humber, and drove off. There was Trivett to think about, Sep Lee, Felicity—and the Spanish girl who had disappeared, the girl he had never seen.

Dawlish reached the narrow street, off Dean Street, at thirteen minutes past ten. The *Liquid Gold* was easily identifiable because a golden bottle, glittering in neon lighting, was hanging outside as a sign to attract the patrons. There were several people in the street, walking couples, two taxis and a private car. Dawlish, his car parked round the corner, walked towards the *Liquid Gold.* A great deal had depended on Sep Lee being trustworthy before; much more depended on it now. If O'Flynn and Charlie Boy could be caught, questioned, forced to talk, then Trivett might see a different side to the picture in the morning.

Sep was standing against a window opposite the restaurant. There was no doubting his identity. Dawlish told himself that the man had a hell of a lot to learn, he shouldn't show himself like that. Would he, if he were playing a crooked game? If he knew anything about a plot like this and how to play it, would he be standing there?

Dawlish was only thirty yards away from him, on the other side of the road, when a door opened close to Dawlish. That happened so swiftly that Dawlish stopped. He saw a small man. He thought it was O'Flynn. He felt a savage blow at his legs, and fell—and heard the roar of a shot at the same time. He struck the pavement, heavily. He saw a flash—and a second. He thought he heard someone shout. A man bent down and smashed a blow at his head which just missed. Another shouted:

"I've got him, I've got him! Mind his gun!"

Then Dawlish knew that he had been framed smoothly—perfectly? He didn't get up, but he could see across the road, he wasn't stone cold as he made out. Sep Lee lay in a crumpled heap, a man was bending over him, somewhere a police whistle was blowing, footsteps thudded nearer, and the man by his side was still shouting:

"Mind his gun!"

Other men were near.

The police were rushing up, and once they held him, that would be that. Then he felt a gun thrust into his pocket, and knew that it would be the murderer's gun.

If he had a chance, this was the moment.

Two men were near him, others were rushing up, and he could make out the shape of a policeman's helmet. But the Humber was only just round the corner, if he could reach that he would stand a chance. If he ran, it would be telling the world that he knew they would find him guilty; but they would, whatever he did.

"*Hold him!*" a man shouted.

"I think—I think he's knocked out," called one of the men. "I'll—I'll try to get—his gun." He sounded as if he were scared, although he believed that the blow on the head had knocked Dawlish out, and had no reason to fear anything. "I think—I think—"

Dawlish moved.

It was like an eruption from a sleeping volcano. One moment he was inert, with a man approaching with pseudo courage and others only a few yards away. Next moment he was on his feet and thrashing out with both arms. He struck one man and sent him flying; another, and crashed him against a window. It broke with a roar that almost deafened everyone near. He heard vague sounds, of shouting, and the piercing note of the police whistle, but no one else got in his way. He raced towards the corner of the street, and round it. The Humber was at hand, but as he reached it, he saw a man straighten up at the other side, and rush away.

He heard a hissing sound.

Intuitively, he ran on, although the police whistle shrilled out again. The hissing sound was air from a tyre, someone had damaged his tyre, probably the valve, to let the air out, to stop him from getting away. Someone meant to make sure that he was held and charged and hanged. It was a kind of vendetta, and he began to think that it was purely personal.

Then he heard a voice, crying:

"Pat!"

Felicity? It couldn't be Felicity, she was at home, she was . . .

"*Pat!*"

It *was* Felicity—Felicity leaning out of an open car door, Felicity waving and shouting, her voice so shrill that it told him of her terror. He reached her as she drew back inside. The nearest pursuers were only thirty yards away when he got in the back. The engine was still running, and Felicity slammed the door and started off. She jarred the clutch. Dawlish thought the engine had stalled. He sprawled in the back, helpless but for her, and fearful; then he heard the engine pick up and the heartening roar. They shot away from the kerb, the engine drowning the other sounds, although he could imagine them all—police whistling, men and women shouting, and others bending over Sep Lee, who was probably dead.

The tyres screamed.

They turned corner after corner.

He straightened up, able to think, now. He saw Felicity, intent on the wheel. No one was after them yet, but the police would use radio, this car would soon be marked down.

"Fel," he said, "slow down when you can, in a side street. I'll jump out. Then start going fast again, it'll give me more time."

"I—what's *happened*?"

"Sep Lee was loyal all right, and Sep's been murdered."

"Sep," Felicity said, in a choky voice. "Trivett's wife—'phoned me. She said that Bill was worried out of his wits because he thought he would have to charge you with murder. Pat, what's happening? What *is* the reason for it?"

"We'll find out. Slow down, my darling. Take that corner."

She took it.

He thought he heard a police whistle, much nearer.

"If you hear from Tim—" he said.

"He 'phoned," Felicity gasped. "Mepita's in Barcelona with her brother, but—"

"That's plenty," said Dawlish, "that's all I wanted to know."

They were going more slowly as they moved along the side street which was near High Holborn. "I'm going to get to Spain. Don't worry. Just be careful, my darling. Be very careful."

He opened the door.

He had hardly a moment to kiss her. He could only jump from the car and then stagger against the window of a shop, making the plate glass boom. He watched the rear light turn the corner. He stepped into a doorway as another car turned into this street and raced in pursuit; a police car.

No one saw him.

Another car flashed by; a third.

He knew that it would not be long before the police caught Felicity. It would not matter, now. He had ten minutes' start, and ten minutes could make the difference between safety and despair.

He had once before been hunted like this; but not with such deadly evidence against him, not with so desperate a cause for fear.

He wanted the docks; a ship for Spain. Where else could he hope to find the key to it all?

CHAPTER XV

THE DOCKS

London's docks were dark, except where a cargo was being loaded or unloaded by the light of flares. There, the winches turned and the cranes groaned and the shrill peep of the foreman's whistle or a flick of his hand controlled the movements of bales of goods or crates of machinery from holds which had been loaded in all corners of the world. Here was the smell of fruit and the smell of meat, or garlic; here were barrels of chestnuts from Genoa and copra from the South Pacific Islands, wool from New Zealand or Australia—food from Europe, wine from France and Italy, from Switzerland and Spain.

Dawlish hovered on the fringe of a floodlit ship, seeing the dark shapes of the men silhouetted against it, some working with a will, some loafing and smoking. Behind him was London and the watchful, searching police, a dead Corez, Sep Lee and a frightened Felicity, who was probably being questioned by the police.

She hadn't told him why she had been there; but he could guess. Trivett's wife had called her, and Felicity had wanted to warn him before he got home, in case the police were there before him. She had known that he was going to the *Liquid Gold.*

He could forget that. . . .

He had to look across the Channel; and further, across the savage wilfulness of the Bay of Biscay, to Vigo, possibly, or much further south to Portugal. He could work his way across France, perhaps, but he had no francs; nothing to help him—except a few English pounds, his watch, his clothes; his purpose. It looked so hopeless that it wasn't worth trying; but he would try.

He saw two men moving towards him, and stepped out of the shadows, so that lights from the dockside fell upon his face. He had taken off his collar and tie, and ruffled his hair and grimed his face.

The men looked at him with little interest.

"Oi, chum," Dawlish said, in a tough voice which wouldn't make them wonder where he came from, "anything leaving for Spain tonight?"

They stopped.

"Watcher wanter know for?"

Dawlish grinned.

"Wouldn't mind a sea trip," he said. "Do me a world o' good." He slipped a ten-shilling note into a not unwilling hand, and then felt the onrush of panic; these men might be dock officials.

They laughed.

"Try the *Spender*," one said, "she's leaving for Vigo and Lisbon, next tide. Or the *Carlos V*, she's a Spanish boat, calling at a dozen ports arter Lisbon. *Spender's* at Number 19, *Carlos V* at 27."

"Chums," said Dawlish, "have a long drink with me."

He walked on.

The police might question them; more probably they were likely to see his photograph in the paper in the morning, and hurry to report what they knew. But there had to be some risks.

He kept in the shadows until he was near the *Carlos V* which was battening down in floodlights. She looked old and very dirty. A Spanish ship would be safer for him than an English one, he decided, and made his way towards it. Dockers were still going up and down the gangway, one of the holds was still open and being loaded. Everything would depend on how much care the look-out men at the head of the gangway took.

He stepped boldly out of the shadow of sheds, crossed railway lines and made his way towards the gangway. Two men came down. He went up, swaying, making himself go as briskly as the others were moving. At the top, two men waited, one English, the other obviously Spanish, wearing a woollen cap and a T-shirt. The Englishman said:

"Where you going?"

"Number 2 hold," Dawlish said promptly.

"Well, make it slippy."

"Okay," said Dawlish.

He found his way down the gangways to the holds. A musty smell came from them; and the smell of sea water and bilge water and oil-cooking and garlic—above everything else, the smell of oil and garlic. He did not go to Number 2 hold, which was being loaded, but to Number 1. Here, it was very dark. He could hear men banging up above; and hear the grinding of the winches and the banging of battens. He squeezed between a car which was fastened by ropes and chocks and some bales of rubber. His hope was that no one would come to the hold until they were at sea. They weren't likely to turn back.

Were they?

It was hot; smelly; tiring. Doing nothing was worse than being on the run. The banging and clattering continued, until he thought that it would never end. He heard the snarling engines all the time, and they did not seem to quicken; but at last something changed. It was quiet. There was a sense of movement, too. Then the siren blew, and he knew they were moving down river, towards the mouth of the Thames and the open sea, then the Channel and—Spain?

Tim Jeremy?

Mepita Fernandez?

His double?

He had a long way to go yet.

He climbed into the car, one door of which was open, and settled as comfortably as he could, although he could not stretch his legs out. He was drowsy, but he kept thinking, asking questions he couldn't answer. Why had it been planned? Who had planned it? Why, who, why, who? Murder and robbery, fencing and framing, it made a crazy picture, but it would end with him standing on the gallows until the trapdoor opened and his neck broke.

Why, why, *why*?

There were those who called Timothy Jeremy a handsome man and others, startled, who said that they thought that he was plain and almost ugly. The argument had often waxed hot, especially among the fair sex in Tim's days of single bliss. The one person who had stood aloof from all argument, apparently the only one who was not even slightly interested, was Timothy Jeremy.

He was tall and very thin. Now, he was tanned to weathered dark brown by the Spanish sun. He had blue-grey eyes which contrasted remarkably with the dark Spanish eyes about him. He sat, alone, in the lounge of the Hotel Toledo, in Barcelona, on a very warm day. Now and again, he fanned himself with a week-old newspaper. Most of the time he looked at the men and women coming in. His wife—who had gone to stay with friends—had expressed some nervous fears at leaving him alone for so long, for Spanish women had a beauty of face and figure which, she said, was likely to tempt a saint himself, and her husband wasn't a saint.

With this edict, Tim had humbly concurred.

He was, however, a worried man.

He was especially worried because only two hours ago, Felicity Dawlish had been on the telephone, asking with desperate hope whether he had heard from Pat. He hadn't. Possibly—probably—Pat had stowed away. It was a week and a day since Dawlish had left London, and Tim knew that some of the cargo vessels called at many small ports and took not days but weeks to cover the coast. There were no grounds for saying that Dawlish was late; but Felicity felt sure that he was, and was very close to despair.

A couple came in, and for a moment Tim thought that the man was like Dawlish; then he decided that it was a mistake and relaxed.

He had been looking for a man who might be mistaken for Dawlish for a long time. He had hunted in dives of the lowest kind to nightclubs of the highest. He had visited every hotel and most of the restaurants. He had become almost a well-known figure in Barcelona, with his photograph of Dawlish and his reasonably smooth question, framed in Spanish:

"Do you know this man?"

A few said that they had seen the man, but no one seemed to be sure. He had almost given up.

Then he saw Mepita Fernandez.

Although he had once seen her entering her apartment with her brother, this was the first time he had seen her on her own. The luck had to break sometimes; perhaps it had broken now. He didn't get up, but watched her with increasing excitement. She was more than something, she was that rarity, a woman whose beauty was wholly serene.

There seemed to be *good*ness in her.

Unexpectedly, Tim had found that expression of goodness, or serenity, on many faces here, among the squalor and the poverty—as well as among the wealthy. But this girl had something which was exclusively hers. Everyone else in the world might have a double but not Mepita. He was quite sure of that.

Then a man joined her.

He looked like Dawlish.

The man who looked like Dawlish most certainly wasn't Dawlish; but the likeness was there, and to strangers it must seem remarkable. It made Tim gape. The man had the same profile, with the flattened nose, the same broad forehead, sloping slightly backwards, the same massive and aggressive chin. The little scar was so noticeable it might almost have been painted on. He wasn't so huge as Dawlish but he was a big man, six feet one or two; and he looked down on Mepita as if on someone who really mattered to him.

They met.

They spoke and Mepita's eyes lit up; and then the light faded from them. Tim got up and went nearer. He knew a little Spanish, but it did not greatly help him then, for Mepita and the man who looked like Dawlish spoke very quickly. He thought that there was reproof and reproach in the girl's voice, but he couldn't be sure. The man appeared to be trying to pacify her.

After a while, he decided that Mepita was not reluctant; she wanted to be pacified.

Tim wished vainly he knew what they were saying.

Then, as he strained his ears, a page boy in a smart cerise uniform came up to him, saluted, and said in careful English:

"Telefono for the mister."

"Eh? Oh! Telephone?"

"Telefono," said the boy, and then was visited by an inspiration, "for the sir."

"I see," said Tim. "All right, thanks. The nearest one, please." He was quite sure that the lad did not understand him. He followed, glancing at Mepita and the man who was like Dawlish. They were on a couch, talking briskly and, he thought, holding hands.

"Telefono," said the boy, beaming, "for the sir, mister."

"Yes," said Tim. "Thanks." Perhaps the boy understood after all, for the booth was almost opposite Mepita and her boy friend. Tim could watch them as he talked. He lifted the receiver, and after some trifling difficulty with the language, made the exchange operator understand who he was.

This caller could be Joan, his wife; or friends in Barcelona; or . . .

"Tim Jeremy speaking."

"Tim," said Dawlish, "I hope you've put your hands on some pesetas, I'm flat broke."

Tim caught his breath. Here was the call he had been waiting for, come at the very worst moment it could. But Dawlish was alive and in good voice.

"Tim!" exclaimed Dawlish, when Tim didn't answer.

"Yes," Tim said. "I heard. The palpitations you can hear are my heartfelt expressions of relief. Where are you?"

"I'm in a big square among the fountains and the pigeons," Dawlish said, "there's a milling mass of trams and traffic and a street called Gracias or something. Can you—"

"Stay there," Tim said, "I'll get there as soon as I can. But not too soon. Believe it or not, I've just seen your double. Amazing how everything has to happen at once, isn't it?"

"Nice work," breathed Dawlish, "don't lose him now. Whatever you do, don't lose him now. I'll wait here for you, you stick to him. All clear?"

His voice was as firm and his purpose as fixed as ever, whatever had happened to him and whatever threat hung over his head. Perhaps he didn't know it all; perhaps he didn't know the worst. Tim Jeremy said yes, he understood—and then saw Mepita and the other man get up.

"They're on the move," he said hastily, "I'll be seeing you."

He rang off, and went out, and followed the man who looked like Dawlish to the door, and beyond.

CHAPTER XVI

THE WORST . . .

It was nearly dark.

The pigeons, which had been clucking and flapping, waddling and occasionally even flying about the great Plaza de Cataluna in the centre of Barcelona, were now cooing as they found the branches of the trees, their perches for the night. People strolled across the square, treading on the peas and the bread and the corn which had been left by the over-fed birds who moved so arrogantly among the hungry poor who fed them. Someone was playing with clappers, far off. Traffic went in a constant whirligig, trams and private cars at what seemed wild speed. Lights were coming on, advertising wines and sherries and whisky and blazoning strange names upon the starlit night.

Huge crowds drifted across the square or sat on the canvas or the wooden seats and chattered idly; and small children, not fearing the wrath of a policeman, dared to beg; and were encouraged by pesetas dropped into grimy hands. All this, Dawlish had observed for a long time past, and was growing tired. It was two hours since he had spoken to Tim; since he had come at last to the end of the road; or so he had hoped. To hear a friendly voice had been a delight; a nectar of a sound. He had travelled so slowly, or so it had appeared, and dared so much, that it had seemed likely that Tim wouldn't be there.

Dawlish could still feel the tension of waiting for him to come to the telephone; and the excitement of hearing what he had said.

Dawlish walked across the square again, searching everywhere for Tim. Now and again he heard American voices; once, he heard an Englishman speak. The rest were the amiable, smiling Spanish. No Tim. Just the milling crowd, all going somewhere but none of them seeming to know where; the flashing lights; the distant stars. And the past. . . .

Dawlish had much more to recall, now.

There was the fiery Spanish captain who had seemed unable to believe that he had a *stowaway*; a man who looked as if he would scream "Clap him in irons" and mean it; or who would have the skin off his back with a rope's end. There had been the second mate, a villainous-looking creature who had spoken a kind of English, pleaded with the skipper, and won. There was the night, the second night out, when they had all been drunk in the captain's cabin, and the captain had started to dance when the waves of the Bay of Biscay, still until then, had decided that it was time they took part; the captain's antics had become so weird and wonderful that Dawlish had collapsed in hopeless laughter.

There had been the passing of his watch and five English pounds; a dinghy alongside from a little port; a swift, urgent row to the rocky shore; the shore itself, a thousand pesetas for ten English pounds, and a cross-country journey which had almost broken his heart—but he had made it.

Then in Barcelona he had found an English newspaper lying in the gutter, dated six days ago, with a headline which read:

DAWLISH STILL AT LARGE

and a few lines beneath it, signifying nothing; and the rest torn off, the only part of the page which had been missing. Then he had found a telephone booth and called Tim, and waited almost breathlessly, and was still waiting.

A shadowy figure loomed.

"Anyone here heard of anyone here named Patrick Dawlish?" Tim Jeremy asked. Powerful fingers gripped Dawlish's arm from behind; the deep voice was a rumble, with laughter in it as well as a measure of relief and satisfaction. "Alive, too. Hungry?"

"I'm fed." They walked side by side. "Find out where he lives?"

"Yes. Talk about a one-track mind."

"I need a one-track mind."

"There, I agree with you," declared Tim Jeremy. He fell silent for a moment. "What do you look like when there's light? Shaved, or—"

"Respectable. I bought a rucksack and I'm a mad English hiker."

"Just a mad Englishman," Tim said. "Let's go and have a drink. If only there were beer, I could face it better." He led the way across the wide road and the dashing trams and reckless cyclists, along a side street which was nearly dark and into a little café where there were mostly men. In the background, a dancer was stamping and clappers were clattering and an unseen crowd was beating time to the unseen dance.

Tim selected a corner.

"I doubt if anyone speaks English, but keep your voice low. Vino," he said to a waiter, and explained earnestly: "Rouge. I mean red." The waiter, refusing to be baffled, beamed and went off. "Pat," said Tim, "I'm glad to see you."

"Where did he go? What's his name? Who was he with?"

"After taking Mepita to her brother's flat on the Avenida Republica, to a place near the docks, just on the fringe of the old town," said Tim. "Narrow streets and crooked windows and odoriferous alleys. I don't know, except that the girl called him Patrick. Mepita."

All this, Dawlish understood.

"How long will it take us to get to the place where 'Mr. Dawlish' is?" he asked, softly.

"Pat," said Tim, "wait. You may be impatient, and I don't blame you, but you still have to be careful. You have," he went on, slowly, firmly, "to be much more careful than you think. Ah, *vino!*" He beamed at the black-haired, bold-eyed waiter, who flourished a bottle of red wine and glasses. The wine looked as if jewels had been distilled and the potion allowed to fall, drop by drop, into the bottle. "*Gracia,*" he said, firmly. "See you later." He turned back to Dawlish, who was sitting very still. "It'll be good," he said. "Here's to the death of your double!"

They drank.

"What's worse?" asked Dawlish. "I know the police were on the rampage for me."

"Rampage? Stampede, you mean. The trouble was," Tim went on, looking first into the ruby red wine then into the cold blue of Dawlish's eyes, next at the stone wall of the restaurant, and the rising smoke, and the bar, "the trouble was that Sep Lee didn't die. The bullet only creased him. He was as right as a Triv—I mean as rain within an hour. Garrulous, too. He said that he was a loyal man, that he could stand everything and anything but *not* ingratitude."

Tim stopped, and examined a man and a girl who had just come in. She was not remarkable, except for her outstanding bosom. . . .

"Tim," said Dawlish, "stop burbling."

"Yes," said Tim. He looked Dawlish full in the eyes. "I see what you mean. Sep Lee is turning Queen's evidence. You and he have worked this racket together since Maurice Gale went away, he says. You started it. You blackmailed him into helping. You keep the lion's share. So he says. So it proceeds, Pat," went on Tim Jeremy very slowly and awkwardly, "he's a goddamned liar but I'm told that he sounds convincing and that it could send you down for a long long time, if not to the last long drop. Sorry. 'Nother spot?"

Dawlish picked up his glass, sipped it, drained it, and held it out for another. He looked at the flowing wine—and it looked like flowing blood, purified by some magic distillation. He stared at the full glass, aware that Tim was watching him intently—and aware of many other things. First, Felicity and what she must be feeling; the agony of her distress. Second, Trivett, and his few friends at the Yard who would hate all this and yet be able to do nothing about it. Third, Sep Lee and his lies; his perjury; his readiness to give false testimony knowing that it was likely to send another man to the gallows. Sep, with his fair Saxon complexion and his dark Spanish eyes, his casual manner—how right Felicity had been.

"I know," Tim said, out of the blue of despair. "A little hell of its own. Still, there's light at the end of the tunnel, old chap. Not bright, but a glim. I mean," he went on as Dawlish stared with new, stark interest, "this chap who looks like you, and Mepita, and the little old house in the little old part of the town. Not far from the docks, or did I tell you?"

"You told me."

"I can find it again," Tim said, with hurtful earnestness; it was simply a fact that he had to say something flippant. "Backwards. Blindfold. I've been doing a bit of research among the old town's narrow streets and whatnot, and I can hardly put a foot wrong. Fact. Only thing is, we'll have to be careful. Reconnoitre, and that kind of thing. The police can be vigorous, I'm told."

"Yes," said Dawlish. "So Sep lied and he's fixed me. If only I knew why."

"Cigarette?" asked Tim, brightly. He thrust his case out, then flicked a lighter, making it look as if he were doing something by sleight of hand. "There we are, then. Point is, Pat, what does the reason matter at this stage? How will it help? I know motive often comes in with a bang, but not in this. First find the bad men and then get their motives. After all, they don't need much more motive, do they?"

"Don't they?"

Tim drew very deeply on his cigarette; it crackled. He did not like looking into Dawlish's face, because that face seemed as if it were made of wood. There was no expression in Dawlish's eyes, just dullness. His lips were set tightly, he didn't move.

"Well, ask yourself. Ready-made stooge to suffer from their villainy. Why not? Get a man who looked like you, and while that's not easy it's not difficult. Remember he was always seen by night or in a poor light, no one ever had a clear dekko at the chap. Your name was mentioned, it looked like you, *hey presto!* and the underworld decided that you had taken it to its bosom. There was the crook, sitting pretty. Once trouble blew up, you'd be on the receiving end and all he had to do was vanish. Vamoose. Fade out. Disappear," added Jeremy, with that tense inanity which he called upon to cloak his feelings. "The puzzle is why it blew up the way it did. Chap's major mistake was marrying in your name. I mean, he might have got away with everything else but should have known that he couldn't get away with that."

"Can't he?"

"Dear old boy," said Tim, "here we are, two of the old brigade, ready to do or die. It's just a case of reconnoitring."

Dawlish stared. . . .

Dawlish began to smile, very faintly at first. Tim gulped and finished his wine. Dawlish's smile became more free, his lips curved, there was even a glint in his eyes.

"Tim," he said, "you're right. I have just had an idea." He chuckled. It was good to see the change in his expression, and Tim Jeremy looked as if it would not take much to make him burst into song. "First, a square meal. Then a look round the old town you're so familiar with. Then a visit to Mepita Dawlish, *née* Fernandez. Your job to make sure that her brother isn't there when I go to see her."

"Well," began Tim, "maybe."

"That's how it's going to be," Dawlish said firmly. "We'll work on Mepita. After all, I haven't seen her yet, have I?"

Tim looked harassed.

"And what are the objections?" Dawlish asked.

"Just the girl," confessed Tim. "Point is, you haven't seen her. So you won't believe that she looks—oh, hellions let loose and to the wall with mushy sentiment! She looks *good*, Pat. You know—as a child can look good."

"And underneath all that, have the soul of the Devil," said Dawlish softly.

They ate well, extremely well, at a restaurant in a narrow side street off the Ramblas. They left the restaurant a little after nine o'clock, and walked, with thousands of others, along the wide street, past the colourful bookstalls, beneath the leafy trees where ten thousand times ten thousand birds perched for the night. Trams clattered on either side as they took the main promenade—and neither of them looked about very much.

Dawlish did not think beyond the night's visit.

He seemed unaware of the possibility that they were followed, and did not once look round. That worried Tim. Dawlish, the real Dawlish, took no chances, and knew all the tricks in the game. True, he had always worked on hunches and it was surprising how often one had come off, but this time—it was too dangerous, too deadly to leave to hunches. Yet that was the way Dawlish was working. He seemed to take no account of the possibility that he had been seen and recognized, and that those who wished him dead in England would be just as eager to see him dead here. The simple fact was that someone had built up a great reputation for buying stolen goods, in his name; and killed in his name; and if he, Patrick Dawlish, suffered the supreme penalty, then the real killer, the real fence, the real 'husband' of Mepita, would be able to come out of hiding and be as free as the air, to live on his ill-gotten gains.

Dawlish knew that it was clever, granted it, but still wondered why he had been selected.

They left the wide street, and went down another so narrow that two people could not pass with comfort. Here, in the Casco Antiguo, lights shone at the windows of tiny shops and strange odours floated into the street. They passed a corner building where chickens were being barbecued, turning slowly on their spits over a charcoal fire which glowed fierce red; and over the doorway was a sign of a snail. They turned right, left, and right again. Above their heads the roofs of the houses seemed to meet. Wraith-like figures hurried to and fro. No one appeared to be interested in them, no one spoke to them, yet Jeremy was not at ease, because Dawlish walked on as if he could only see what lay ahead, and gave no thought to the perils which might spring from behind.

Tim saw no one.

They came to a junction of narrow, cobbled roads, and in the centre of these crossroads, a great nuisance to all traffic, stood a small fountain. Here, they stopped. Small boys and young women went to the fountain and put their mouths beneath the ever-flowing stream of water.

"The second house along," Tim said. "That's where your double went to, Pat. If I were you I'd wait until everyone else has gone to bed, and then visit this place. Bound to be a way we can break in. You can put the fear of Patrick Dawlish into the chap. If I know you you'd have him talking so loudly that they could hear it in London. Now Mepita—"

"What we need," said Dawlish, "is someone who can speak the lingo, telephone Carlos Fernandez, get him out of his flat so that Mepita's left there alone. Who do you know?"

"I never could be doing with the one-track mind," Tim said with a sigh. "I'll call a friend and lay it on. But how are we going to lure Fernandez out of his flat?"

Dawlish grinned in the sultry light of the night.

"Tell him I'm here and want a chat with him before going to the police," he said. "He'll come running."

Tim Jeremy did not say so, but obviously he did not feel sure.

CHAPTER XVII

MEPITA

Dawlish stood beneath the trees on the Avenida Republica. It was nearly midnight. There was some traffic, but it was not thick or noisy; just fast. A few people hurried past him; no one dawdled. The street lamps in the great avenue were on, shining among the trees, on to the closed shops and the massive buildings on either side. The avenue was so wide that it was almost a journey to cross it; there were service roads as well as the main thoroughfare. A few cars were parked in these service roads.

He watched Number 698.

Tim had told him that this was an apartment building, and that the Fernandez family—now just Carlos, although Mepita had a room there—had a top-floor flat. There was a lift, self-operated.

He didn't move; had the trick of stillness and of silence which had lured many hapless people to disaster.

Then a man hurried out of Number 698.

Dawlish kept quite still, but his lips moved as he smiled. That was Carlos Fernandez, his darkly handsome face clear in the lamplight. Fernandez turned right, towards the centre of the city and walked very fast. He kept walking, and was out of sight when Dawlish reached the other side of the road—and the doorway of Number 698.

He was alone.

Tim was an invisible one-man reception party for Fernandez, who had undoubtedly fallen for the invitation. Tim would follow the Spaniard. There was a possibility that Fernandez had telephoned his friends for help, of course. The risk had to be taken, and Tim cheerfully took it.

Dawlish pushed open a small wrought iron gate inside a massive, barred iron gate, and stepped into the smooth court-yard of the building. A gentle wind rustled through the branches of trees and shrubs. A dim light shone inside the vast hallway, approached by a flight of stone steps. It was more like a mansion than a block of flats.

Dawlish went up, pushed the door, stepped inside. Here, a stone floor was covered with huge pieces of rush matting. A sign over a doorway said *Lift*. He went towards it. The building was silent, almost uncanny in its soundlessness—and when he pressed the button and the lift came down, the noise seemed an affront.

The lift stopped.

Dawlish stepped in; and was taken up slowly.

A light burned on the top floor, too, soft and subdued. There were four flats, two approached along narrow passages on either side of the hall. Mepita's flat was on the right. Dawlish walked towards it. Here the floor was of cement with no covering, and it was difficult not to make some sound.

He reached the door, and stood amid the silence. Then he took out some tools which Tim had provided from the tool-kit of the car.

He studied the lock.

It was a Yale; he could get it open although he could not

fasten it again; so that anyone who came here would find the door unlocked. That was another risk to take, he couldn't just ring the bell, for Mepita might not be alone. She was married, wasn't she? Even if her brother had gone rushing away, the man who looked like Dawlish might have come here.

There were faint scratching sounds as Dawlish worked.

No other noise came.

Then the lock clicked back.

Dawlish pushed the door gently, and it swayed open, and light came through—light from a room with an open door. He stepped inside. He heard nothing at all. He pushed the door to, gently, and then pulled up a chair and placed it against the wood, so that if anyone tried to get in they would be bound to push the chair, and would raise some kind of alarm.

Dawlish crossed the hall.

The carpet was soft and yielding underfoot. The poor light was just sufficient to show signs of luxury; there was an atmosphere about this place which no one could escape.

Dawlish reached the partly open door.

He pushed it a little wider, and peered inside.

Mepita was staring at him, eyes rounded and starry with fright, lips parted, one hand at her breast, the other thrust forward, with a gun in it.

She was only a yard away from the telephone in a corner.

"Hallo, Mepita," greeted Dawlish softly, "what a way to greet your husband!"

He smiled at her. He had a smile which could melt a thousand hearts; more often than not, it could melt Felicity's when she was in a white heat of temper about some piece of idiocy.

Mepita stared at him, her mouth opening wider, the gun drooping.

"You know," said Dawlish, very gently, "you're quite lovely. You're about the loveliest thing I've ever seen."

He was close to her.

"Go—go *away*," she breathed.

"Soon," said Dawlish, and stretched out his hand. "Give me the gun."

This was the fateful moment, when fear might make her squeeze the trigger. She couldn't miss. There was just a single, palpitating moment of danger; she didn't squeeze. With a lightning swift movement Dawlish struck the gun aside. Before she could recover, he grabbed it, held it, and backed away.

"Thank you, Mepita *mia*," he said.

She stared as if she were looking at some hideous and unbelievable creature from another world. There had been fear; now, her chief emotion was horror, perhaps with some astonishment. She could not believe the evidence of her eyes, and was as still as Dawlish, but breathing deeply, gustily.

She was dressed in a black suit, with a white blouse. She looked virginal. Her beauty was not of this world, and the glossy brightness of her brown eyes made them look like lamps burning with some inner fire. Her hair was a cluster of black curls, shiny and black as a raven's wing. Her complexion was a dream, smooth and peach-like; every feature was perfect. She was perfection of face and figure, and no one—man, woman or child—could ever doubt it.

She did not move, once he had taken the gun.

"Hallo, Mepita," Dawlish said again, "I'm Patrick Dawlish."

She gave just a catch of her breath and a swift, impulsive flutter of her hands, as if she were thrusting a vision away from her.

"*No*," she breathed.

"Yes," said Dawlish.

"Oh, no, it cannot be," she prayed. "He told me—"

She stopped. She swayed. Dawlish moved forward, very quickly. She would not have fallen, but she seemed glad of help. He took her to a chair and helped her to sit down, then moved away and smiled, knowing that she might be made in the mould of Delilah, yet tempted to believe in her innocence just because of her looks.

"What did he tell you, Mepita?"

How her eyes glistened!

"Carlos told me—you were—*dead.*"

"Not yet by a long, long way," said Dawlish. "I think Louis will die before me, yet. Do you know why he married you in my name?"

"No, no, I do not," she said. Her breathing was very swift, laboured, frightened; he knew that the shock of seeing someone so like her husband added to the shock of finding a stranger in the flat. "But his passport, I see it! Also, mine is made good for me as Mrs. Dawlish."

"So he had a forged passport, too," Dawlish said softly. "I'm sorry, Mepita. He's a very nasty piece of work."

She said: "What—do you say?"

"The man you—married is a very bad man."

"Oh, no," she said, "no." But she spoke utterly without conviction. She closed her eyes, and for a moment Dawlish looked down on troubled beauty and found it hard to believe that such a woman was really there, in the flesh.

"*No,*" she breathed, "Carlos would not lie to me."

"Carlos probably believed Louis was really me," Dawlish said; but he wondered. "What has Carlos discovered now?"

"He—he says that my husband was in some trouble, he could not use his own name, so he used the name of another *Dawlish,*" she breathed. "You—you are so like—my husband."

"So I'm told," said Dawlish. "It's my bad luck."

He wasn't getting anywhere very fast, knew that he would have to fight his surging impatience. It wasn't easy. The most difficult thing was to realize that he was in the presence of a girl who seemed to have so simple a faith in man, who was so naïvely innocent.

Could she be? Could anyone be?

"Is he—safe?" Mepita asked. "Understand, I will not hurt him, I—" she broke off, as if too bewildered to think clearly. She had married a man who had lied to her and fooled her, and she was only just beginning to realize all that it might mean.

Would she talk?

If he gave her time to think, she probably wouldn't; but she was still suffering from shock, and he might be able to make her tell the truth—or that part of the truth that mattered. He stepped nearer, and spoke in a matter-of-fact voice which did nothing to reflect the emotions raging in him.

"Listen, Mepita," he said, "I don't know what it's all about, but I do know that your brother is in trouble now, that you are, that this man called Louis is responsible. But—" he smiled that expansive winning smile, and hoped that it would fool her for long enough—"it may not have been Louis's fault. He may need help. I can't help him if I don't know what happened, can I?"

"*Will you* help him?"

"Why not?" asked Dawlish. "I want to know the truth, that's all, just the simple truth. Why did you marry him, Mepita?"

She answered at once:

"Because I fell in love with him." She hesitated, then went on as if talking in a dream. "Never before had I been in love. He came to see Carlos, but Carlos was away. So, he talked to me. He gave me a beautiful ring, it was very, *very* beautiful." She played with a ring on her finger, but did not look down at it. "He told me that he was a jewel merchant, and he travelled to many countries on his business, and—he *did.* That was not a lie, it was the truth."

"Yes," said Dawlish, gently.

"At the time Carlos is in trouble," Mepita went on, abruptly. "He takes money which belongs to friends, he spends it, he needs money urgently." She had dropped into the present tense as if she were living through those days again. "So, I agree to sell my jewels, and who would sell them better than Louis whom I call Pat-rick?"

"No one," agreed Dawlish solemnly.

"So, he takes them, but the money does not come, and Carlos does not meet my husband, is very worried," said Mepita. "Then we hear from Pat-rick. He is in London, he cannot come to Spain for some weeks and cannot send the money, but says he will bring it. There is not time for that, though. I decide to go and see him. He is very surprised, of course. Then Carlos, who hurried to come before me, and stays at the hotel, fetches me from my husband's house. He finds out about this wrong name, this Louis not Patrick, but he tells me only tonight, here in Barcelona. Before this, he did not want me to be hurt. But tonight he tells me there is nothing he can do or I can do. Louis is—is in trouble, also, there is some talk about stolen jewels. I have talked to Louis about it! He did not know they were stolen. He did not *know.*"

Her voice faded away.

In her heart she knew that the man who had lied about his name had also lied about the jewels. She was sure that he was a thief; a dealer in stolen gems. All these things had been forced into her mind, and she was sick at heart. There was fear for her brother, too—it seemed easy to see how she was suffering.

Or was this all put on, for his benefit? She might be fooling him, as Sep had. Dawlish hated to suspect that; no one, looking into her lovely face and the purity of her expression, could easily believe that there was evil in her.

"What made you leave London so quickly?" he demanded.

"Carlos is told that everything he has done will be told to the police if he does not return at once to Spain, and say nothing of what has happened there. I do not know who said that." She must guess, though—her 'husband' had wanted her out of the country. "It was clear that someone did not want Carlos and me to see you, the real Pat-*rick*." So she was facing up to the wicked truth. "I must be prevented from seeing you, so—we are sent back. That is when I begin to wonder about—my husband."

Dawlish didn't speak.

"At the hotel where I go to see Carlos, a man comes to see me," she went on. "He wants a photograph that there is of—of my husband and me when we are in Paris together. On—our honeymoon."

There was a tense moment—and then she seemed to fall forward. She buried her face in her hands and she began to cry.

Dawlish stood watching her; wanting to believe in her.

At heart, she knew all the truth. More, she knew that there was a man, very much like him, who had dealt in stolen jewels. He could take Mepita with him to the police, and once her story had been told, he would be free from suspicion. She was a vital witness for him; and, therefore, a vital, a dangerous witness against this other man; and the Blonde Doll; and all who were involved.

He must get her away from here, soon. Now.

He watched her shoulders shaking and listened to her sobbing—and then he heard a different sound. In a flash, he was alert; and the sound was repeated, he knew that someone else was trying to enter the apartment.

CHAPTER XVIII

CORPSE

Dawlish turned away from Mepita.

He tip-toed towards the door. Her sobs came quietly, she was fighting to restrain the paroxysm; but she might drown the sound that the newcomer had made.

Dawlish reached the door of the room.

The chair was still against the front door, but it had moved a few inches. A man's arm was stretched inside the door; fingers clutched the chair, and began to push it back slowly. It was a long arm, the hand was long and pale, too; and the man wore a cream linen coat.

Dawlish tip-toed across the hall.

The door slid back, making little sound. He could still hear the girl crying.

He stood in another room doorway as this door was pushed open wide enough for a man to squeeze through. The stealthiness of the other's movements told their own story. Dawlish held Mepita's automatic in his right hand, and watched as the man put his head round the door.

It was a man with thick-lensed glasses, a pale face, a snub nose.

He had been in Withy Street, once, and near the Litton Hotel later, the man whom Allison had followed. Now, he squeezed through, and stood by the door, looking towards the open door. He could probably see Mepita with her shoulders bowed.

She was almost quiet, now.

The man moved towards the doorway, with his right hand at his pocket. He drew it out, slowly; and he also carried a gun. He glanced round once or twice, as if he weren't at ease; but he was intent on the room and the girl in there, obviously nothing else really mattered.

He reached the door.

He levelled the gun.

In that moment Dawlish knew that the man was going to kill Mepita, that he had come here for that purpose. She could give evidence that would detsroy the whole plot, and so she had to die. It might be another step in the framing of Dawlish, too, the crooks might know that he had come here; or expect him soon.

If they knew that he was in Barcelona, they would know that he would be suspected of the murder of the girl.

All those things flashed through Dawlish's mind in a split second of time—while the man with the thick-lensed glasses and the snub nose took careful aim at the unsuspecting girl. Once he squeezed the trigger, she would die.

Dawlish fired at him.

The shot roared, reverberating about in the apartment, the girl cried out in sudden terror. The man kept still, then dropped his gun. Mepita screamed again; she was staring at the man, who began to crumple up. The bullet had caught him in the back. He just fell, as his knees bent; hit the floor with a thud, and pitched forward.

Mepita's screams were high-pitched, frightening, terrifying.

Dawlish called: "Be quiet!" He moved towards the door, stepped over the fallen man, saw her sitting in that large armchair, staring, eyes rounded, lips forming an O which almost distorted her lovely face. "*Be quiet!*" breathed Dawlish, and reached her in two strides, thrust a hand over her mouth, stifling the next scream.

He felt her teeth slide over the palm of his hand.

He felt her body quivering.

He waited tensely, fearful that someone else had heard the shooting and the screaming.

No sounds came. Perhaps no one was in the neighbouring apartments.

Dawlish looked at the man with the thick-lensed glasses, who was lying with his head towards him, his right hand a few inches from his gun. There was a red stain on the left side of his coat, below the shoulder-blade. The jerk of the gun against Dawlish's pocket had diverted the bullet.

Dawlish eased his grip of Mepita.

"He was going to shoot you," he said. "Be quiet."

She didn't speak or scream, and he took his hand away. She breathed shudderingly. He still listened intently for sounds from neighbouring apartments, but heard nothing; but it did not prove that no one had heard the screaming and the shooting. He bent over the wounded man, felt his pulse, was sure that he was dead. This was another reason why he had to get away; but if she were left here with the dead man, if she were left here at all, sooner or later she would have to tell the police what had happened.

All was silent.

Dawlish turned to look at the girl.

"Mepita," he said, "understand this. He was going to shoot

you. He was going to kill you, because you can tell the difference between your husband and me. Do you understand? You are a vital witness in a case of murder."

She caught her breath. "Yes. Yes, I see."

"And you're in danger. So we have to get away. We'll have to move him, too."

"I—I cannot leave—" she began.

He could not even begin to guess what her reaction would be. She was suffering from shock, and shock affected people in a lot of different ways. There was time for her to become hysterical, and she looked as if she might. Or she might faint. Or she might refuse to go because she was expecting her brother.

Seconds were precious to Dawlish. There was still the danger that the shooting and the screaming had been heard; at any moment the police might come.

"All right, Mepita," he said quietly, and moved towards her with a disarming smile. It fooled her. He went behind her, then struck her on the back of the neck, a sharp, expert blow. Her head jerked violently, she gasped and slumped down unconscious.

He used his tie to bind her wrists and a handkerchief to gag her. Then he left her in the chair, slumped forward, and went to the dead man.

The blood was spreading, now, and soaking into the linen coat; none had dripped to the floor.

Dawlish moved him gently; the dead weight was difficult to handle. He felt in all his pockets, took out everything and thrust the oddments into his pockets, including a wallet and a watch. Then he straightened up, and went into another room, a bedroom.

He found a cabin trunk, with a key tied to it.

He lugged this into the hall, opened it, then lifted the dead man and put him inside; he had to bend the other's arms and legs. The sightless eyes, half closed, seemed to mock him. The thick lips were parted, too.

Dawlish closed the trunk; locked it; and stood up, drawing the back of his hand across his forehead. He was wringing with sweat.

He went to the open front door.

No one had appeared; no other lights showed.

He went back, hoisted the trunk to his shoulders, grunting with the effort, and then went towards the lift. Three minutes later, he was downstairs; five minutes later, the trunk was outside, hidden in the shadows of the trees. When he had found Tim, he could come back for it.

But—had the dead man come alone?

No one was near, except a few people who went hurrying by.

No one appeared to watch; but then, Dawlish had not known that the man was in the building until he had heard that telltale sound.

And in that trunk was a man whom he, Dawlish, had *killed*. That was something to remember.

He went back to the lift—and then stopped abruptly. It was moving. He backed swiftly across the hall, but the lift came to a stop and the doors opened and a young man came out. He saw Dawlish, must have seen his features clearly. He stared, as if intrigued, then gave a slight bow and turned towards the door.

So he had been in the building; but would he be so calm if he had heard the shooting?

The doors swung to behind the man, who walked smartly towards the front door.

Dawlish followed very quietly, went into the courtyard, saw the man go through the small gate, then turn right. There was no shout, no whistle, nothing to suggest that he had raised an alarm.

A car door slammed; an engine hummed.

Dawlish turned back towards the lift.

Upstairs, Mepita was still unconscious. Dawlish wasted no time looking at her, but went into the bedroom, searching for papers, for anything which might help him later. He found nothing at all. The search took him ten minutes, and when he had finished, Mepita was coming round.

He unfastened her wrists, and stuffed his crumpled tie into his pocket.

"We're leaving in a hurry," he said. "Do exactly what I tell you, and you'll be all right."

She didn't answer.

He had to pull her from the chair, and she swayed. He made her walk with him into the kitchen, gave her some water, watched her as she gradually recovered her control. But twenty-five minutes had passed since he had come back, before they went to the door. She had a coat round her shoulders, and held her handbag; he had thrust the bag at her, at the last minute.

She hadn't said a word.

"Understand," he said, "do exactly what I tell you."

"I—see," she said at last. Her voice was dull, her eyes were dull; and no one could be surprised. Dawlish kept an arm round her waist and helped her towards the front door. He pulled it to, but it sagged open, and there was nothing at all he could do about that now, without losing more precious time.

He waited at the lift, in a fever of impatience, and Mepita leaned against him, staring at the closed doors. It wasn't until the lift was almost, at floor level that he realized that someone might be in it—coming to visit Mepita, or one of the other tenants.

He clenched his teeth.

The doors opened on to an empty lift.

Outside, the night seemed darker; some street lamps had been switched off. The trunk was still in the shadows. The girl walked mechanically by his side, as if she could no longer think, and was doing everything subconsciously. At least she had given no serious trouble.

Dawlish stepped into the street.

Parked a few yards away was a large American car; he had seen it there before. Now he saw the gleaming, tempting chromium of the bumpers and the bonnet. The idea came as he stood watching. He moved swiftly to the car; the doors were locked, but one ventilation window wasn't quite closed. He worked dexterously, soon had the door open, and sat at the controls. He used a piece of wire for an ignition key; it might work at once, might take him vital minutes.

The ignition light glowed.

"Wait here," he whispered to Mepita.

He left her sitting in the car; he had no choice. He hurried back for the trunk, hoisted it, and hurried back, breathing hard. He unfastened the back door; there was just room to get the trunk inside. Mepita sat staring along the wide thoroughfare as traffic flashed by, most of the cars with headlights on.

Dawlish slammed the door and took the wheel.

He worked the controls, to test them, found out which was which, and pressed the self-starter.

The engine turned.

He switched on the lights—and then he heard a shout, from close by, and an unmistakable American voice.

"Hi, stop there! Stop thief!" Footsteps sounded, very near, and the man kept shouting: "Hi! Hi, stop thief!"

Dawlish slid the car into motion towards the nearest cross road.

Mepita sat stiffly by his side.

CHAPTER XIX

OLD TOWN

Dawlish sent the huge car hurtling along the avenue, headlights blazing for the first few seconds, then using only the parking lights. He saw nothing behind him; no pursuing car. He turned off the broad street towards the left, and took several sharp turns, then found himself back on the Avenida. He didn't know Barcelona at all, although he had studied a map carefully, and he believed that he could find his bearings.

He had to get rid of the trunk, first. Then he could think of Mepita.

He said: "Can you hear me?"

"Yes," she said, in a dull voice.

"We have to get rid of the trunk. Understand—the body. Where shall we take it?"

"There is—the sea," she said. "Or perhaps—a park."

"Tell me where to go," he said brusquely.

If she chose, she could take him straight to the police. He didn't think that she would. He wished there were some life in her, but shock upon shock seemed to have dulled her wits. Were they too dull? Deliberately dull?

She told him to go straight on.

Ten minutes later he turned off the main road, where a sign said Madrid one way, and Sitgas in the other. He took the Sitgas road, and soon Mepita told him to turn off again. He had no idea where they were, but soon he stopped in the darkness, and just discerned a tangle of trees and bushes. She wasn't so dull as he had thought. He tumbled the trunk out and pushed it among the bushes, scratching his head and face and hands.

Satisfied, he turned back.

She sat quite still.

From the road an old man watched, and when the car had gone, went slowly forward to the hidden trunk.

He drove towards the city, and Mepita told him how to approach by a different road. They reached the docks; he could see two ships being worked by floodlight, and the Mediterranean carried his thoughts back to London. They drove alongside a railway, where trains were puffing and blowing and wagons were being shunted, and then she said:

"You are in the Old Town, now."

"The Caracolas?"

"It is ten minutes' walk," she said.

He left the car at the side of the road. His finger-prints would be on it, but he couldn't hope to wipe them all off; and he left them. He watched as they walked away, fearful in case they were noticed by a policeman who might know that a Chrysler had been stolen.

No one stopped them.

Soon, they were approaching the Caracolas, where the chickens still turned on the spit, and people still ate, although very few were in the streets. Tim might not be here yet. Without Tim, he was lost; he had no money, knew no Spanish, and could not rely on Mepita.

A tall figure approached from the restaurant.

"Just follow me," Tim said.

Tim took them to a small hotel. A tired-looking porter who badly needed a shave was sitting at the desk, reading a newspaper; but although he showed no outward interest, he glanced at the trio as they passed. Tim led the way up narrow stairs. There was a smell of oil cooking and of garlic; the smell which had been in Dawlish's nostrils since he had landed.

They went up two flights.

"Here we are," said Tim. "Perfect spot, eh?"

Neon lights outside were flashing on and off, and brightening the room. Tim closed the door, and switched on the lights. Dawlish closed his eyes in the glare. Mepita moved away from him. When he saw her he realized that her eyes looked glassy and she still gave the impression that she was moving in a trance.

"Take it easy, now," Tim said gently. He led the girl to an armchair and helped her to sit down; as Dawlish had done, earlier. "Keep to the side of the window," he said to Dawlish. "And look."

Dawlish obeyed.

The fountain in the middle of the crossroads was still playing, but no one drank at it. Just across the narrow street was the house which Tim had pointed out before—the house where the man who looked like Dawlish and called himself Louis had gone to. It couldn't be more than six feet away.

Tim was smug. "Not bad," he said.

"Wonderful."

"Don't make it sound like a dirge," reproved Tim, and glanced at Mepita. "Won't she talk?"

"Where's Carlos?"

"He turned up, as expected," said Tim. "He fumed for half an hour or so, then sallied forth to a telephone booth. After that, he came here. I followed him all the way. Unless he left while I was waiting at the Caracolas, he's still inside. I don't know about Louis the Dawlish Double, but he's probably there too. Pat, why the gloom?"

"With Mepita, nervous shock. With me—" Dawlish took the automatic out of his pocket, and looked at it. "It works," he said. "I've just killed a chap and dumped his body. Not a nice chap, he was going to kill Mepita, but it isn't so good."

There was a long, tense pause. Then:

"So *good*," echoed Tim. "You're not safe out on your own. You—" he breathed explosively.

"Easy, Tim!"

"Ah, yes," said Tim, quietening. "I understand. Sorry." He watched as Dawlish emptied his pockets on to a small table. Mepita also watched; she had not stirred since Tim had helped her into the chair. "Loot?" asked Tim. He turned over two or three of the oddments—a pen, some keys, a small steel pocket watch—while Dawlish opened the dead man's wallet.

There was nothing to help them, but one thing of interest—a photograph of a woman. It was dog-eared and cracked in several places, but it didn't wholly destroy the likeness. The woman was youngish, nice-looking in a bold way, and fair-haired.

"Blonde Doll," remarked Tim. "Didn't you mention her?"

"Yes."

"Funny thing," said Tim.

"What's funny?"

"I seem to have seen her before."

"She's a type."

"Something more than that," declared Tim. "I could swear—" he broke off, shrugging. "Not that it helps much. That the lot?"

"He's got a few thousand pesetas," Dawlish said.

"Don't be ghoulish."

Dawlish drew a sharp breath, and looked up into Tim's lean, brown face. For a moment, he was absurdly angry; trying to ease the tension, Tim had only worsened it. They stared like that for several seconds; then Dawlish relaxed, and actually chuckled.

"Thanks," said Tim, and eased his collar. "Apologies."

"Just what I need," said Dawlish, "it's got too tense. Life's still life. You didn't think to send a message to Fel, did you?"

"Oh, but I did—I got one of my Spanish friends to telephone her," said Tim. "Took a chance that the line at your flat is tapped. The message was simply, 'Safe, don't worry', so it didn't give anything away."

"No. Thanks." Dawlish lit a cigarette. "Meet my new wife," he said, and looked at Mepita with great sympathy, then went towards her. "It will work out, Mepita," he said gently, "and you've been very, very good,"

She said: "Where is Carlos?"

"With Louis, I think."

"They must *not* hurt Carlos."

Dawlish didn't speak.

"They must not hurt my brother," she said, and sat up more erect. "You must make sure of that." She hardly knew what she was saying; just the one thing mattered, making sure that Carlos was not hurt. "*Can you make sure?*"

"No," said Dawlish. "We can only try."

"They will kill him," said Mepita. She stood up, more quickly than she had moved all the evening. It was as if she had found strength from some hidden source, and could walk about again, could think, had full control of her actions and her thoughts. "That man came to kill me, I saw the gun. I know. In that moment, I also know everything. The man Louis is—bad." The word came quietly, but without a note of despair. During the past hours, she had been suffering from the shock of the truth; now she had absorbed it and was ready to fight. "In London, I wonder about him, he is so cross because I go. I do not—love him as I thought I did."

She paused, and her hands were clenched, her body stiff.

"He tries to kill me. He cheats, he robs. And—because of him, Carlos is in danger. How can we help Carlos?"

It was just the attitude he had hoped she would adopt.

Dawlish said: "They'll probably try to strike a bargain."

"How can they? I am not at home, they cannot talk to any of us."

Dawlish said mildly: "I'm going to see them."

She didn't speak, just stared unbelievingly.

"Pat," said Tim, "you aren't carrying enough insurance to do a thing like that."

"I think I am," said Dawlish. "Mepita's the witness who matters. Keep Mepita away from the other side, and they daren't do anything else. We'll stay here. They won't expect us to be on their doorstep."

"And you will really go to see them?" Mepita gasped.

"I think so."

"If they should kill—" she began.

"I know what you mean," conceded Dawlish with a sudden grin. "I've had time to think, too. I haven't a chance to escape, without your evidence. I could try to get you sent to England, but there'd be a lot of trouble, and I might not pull it off. We want Carlos safe and sound, too. Louis might kill on sight, but Louis may suddenly realize that things aren't so good as they were." He lit a cigarette. His expression was wooden now, he looked huge, powerful, and rather dull and very tired. "I'll give them the night to get agitated in, I think. How many rooms did you book, Tim?"

"There's a dressing-room with a single bed," said Tim, pointing. "Mepita can have that. I'll manage with an armchair for a few hours, a bed will be too cosy."

"Sounds all right," said Dawlish, and fought back yawns.

Mepita did not say a word.

Dawn spread over Barcelona, gently, beautifully. The city stirred. Donkey carts with huge iron-shod wheels clattered over the cobbles of the narrow streets near the Casco Antiguo. People began to move to and fro, shops opened early, sleepy voices were raised, children began to laugh. The blind and the halt and the maim left the hovels where they lived and moved towards the main streets, carrying their trays with the tickets of the latest national lottery for sale—their substitute, by the law, for begging. Trams clattered in the distance. Nearer to Dawlish, the water splashed from the little fountain in the road.

Dawlish washed and shaved.

He had looked in to see Mepita, and she was lying asleep with her clothes on but her shoes off and her skirt loosened at the waist. She gave him the impression that she had tossed and turned for hours before she had dropped off, but that now she would sleep the clock round.

Dawlish went to the wardrobe, and took out his suit. The gun was still in the coat pocket. He took it out, broke it, and squinted down.

"Three left," he said.

"You stop this trigger-happy nonsense," Tim advised.

"That's right," agreed Dawlish, "look where it leads you." He put the gun away. "I've done a little thinking as well as a little dreaming, Tim. This is the way to handle it, I think. Bold, dashing methods." He smiled faintly. "I think it will give them a shock, and I think they'll know they daren't move far until they've killed Mepita. She's the great danger to them, and I wouldn't give two pesetas for her life, if they catch up with her."

Tim said brightly: "I'll protect her, Patrick!"

"I know you'll try."

"I also have a gun."

Dawlish said: "I don't know whether we ought to take her somewhere else, first. Some sanctuary. The trouble is that once we lose her, we've lost her for good. At the moment, she'll do pretty well what we say, but if the police get at her—" he stopped.

"I also have been thinking," said Tim, "you're not the only one with little grey cells. You're right, although I hate saying so. The best chance is to go and tackle Louis. I don't know what tactics you'll use, but I can guess."

Dawlish smiled, looking a little less like a wooden giant.

"Guess."

"You'll tell Louis that he's in such a mess that he can't get out by himself. What about a deal? A statement of guilt completely clearing you, and time to get away to some other fair land before you warn the police."

"Right," said Dawlish.

"And if he'll play you'll then promise to turn Mepita over to him," went on Tim. "If you and Louis are hand-in-glove, she's no longer a threat. And you can keep her quiet, anyway, by threatening to put Brother Carlos in quod. Right?"

"Right."

"It's thin," opined Tim. "It's not going to wear well, but it might fool Louis just long enough to give you a chance to break them all up. Right?"

"You're almost omniscient," said Dawlish.

When he left the hotel an hour later, after a breakfast of coffee with too much milk and rolls with too little butter, he walked straight to the main street, past the dead fire, past the barbecue spits but not the chickens, to the trams. He was not followed. He walked to Plaza de Cataluna, where the pigeons were already strutting. Then he took a taxi to the house in the narrow street where, according to Tim, there was the man who had impersonated him. No one had followed.

Now it was really touch and go.

Dawlish did not realize just how narrow a margin he was working on. He knew that he had left his finger-prints on the borrowed American car, knew nothing of a little old man, or the prints on car and trunk and body, that they would be classified so quickly—or that news of them and a clear description of the prints had been cabled to London; or that Superintendent Trivett was, at that very moment, reading the report from Barcelona.

It was a worried Trivett who had been in touch with the Spanish police for several days.

He knew these prints were Dawlish's.

The evidence against Dawlish was building up so strongly that even Trivett was beginning to waver in his faith.

A dead body had been found inside a trunk which was also littered with Dawlish's finger-prints, off a road which led to the sea.

With this news in front of him, Trivett went from his office to the office of his Chief, tapped, and went in. They talked for five minutes, then left together, Trivett with a photograph of the pale-faced man whose body had been found in the trunk.

Trivett took it to Septimus Lee.

CHAPTER XX

SAYS LEE . . .

Septimus Lee looked quite composed as Trivett and the Assistant Commissioner at Scotland Yard entered the waiting-room where he was being held that morning. He would be taken back to his remand cell at Wandsworth as soon as they had finished. His curiously dark eyes looked so strange in his fair face, and against his fair but greying hair. He smiled faintly; and Trivett realized, almost for the first time, how red his lips were; a raw kind of red.

"'Morning, Lee," Trivett said, brusquely.

"Good morning, Mr. Trivett."

"Know this chap?" Trivett asked, and handed over the photograph which had been telephoted and sped from Barcelona during the night. There was the man whom Dawlish had killed, no doubt at all.

"Oh, yes, I know Sam Webber," said Septimus Lee, without a moment's pause. "He was one of the crowd, Mr. Trivett. He never did trust Dawlish—he was against having Dawlish anywhere in the show. And how right he was!"

"Where did Webber live?" asked Trivett, then put the routine questions, with his heart getting heavier and heavier.

An hour later the dead man was identified as Samuel Webber by two other people, and the noose was drawing tighter round Dawlish's neck.

Trivett went to his Chief's office again.

The Assistant Commissioner, severe, flaxon-haired, a whippet of a man, looked down his nose.

"It's a bad business, Trivett. Couldn't be worse. Of course I know what you feel about Dawlish. You've been close friends for years, natural you should have the greatest possible faith in him. Still—evidence is evidence."

"And finger-prints are finger-prints," Trivett murmured.

"Of course, and you understand the situation. We must send someone over to Barcelona at once. In fact, they've asked us to. And it's a very delicate business." The Assistant Commissioner was undoubtedly embarrassed by what he had to say, and gave a curious sound, something like: "*Hrrrrmph!*" Then he gave a smile which was almost a wolfish grin. "There's the probability that our crooks have been sending stolen jewels over to Spain for a long time. Dawlish and his business friends had their selling agency there. Can't tell who else might be involved. All kinds of business houses get suspected, and we don't want more trouble—have enough as it is." The A.C. went "*hrrrmph!*" again. "The quicker it's cleared up the better, and I'd like you to go over yourself. Take Pottle with you, or anyone you like. And—ah—bring Dawlish back if you can. We may have to leave him, though, for trial there. Still, do all you can."

Trivett said formally: "Very good, sir."

"Sorry it has to be you." The A.C. was wolfish again. "There it is."

There was much more than that to be said, Trivett knew. Rumour could be an ugly thing, and there were whispers that he had deliberately let Dawlish go, or at least, had given Dawlish too much rope. The A.C. knew all about them, and the A.C. was being very decent—offering him the task of dealing with Dawlish and so giving the lie to the rumours.

There it was.

Trivett called Pottle, who jumped at the chance to go, and was as glad of a chance of getting at Dawlish.

"Get the tickets for the first available 'plane," Trivett said. "And I mean the first one."

It was then half past ten.

At half past two, he was sitting in the 'plane at the London airport, looking back at the airport buildings, when he saw a woman running towards the 'plane. They waited for her. She drew nearer. It was a small window, and rather misty on the outside, but not so obscured that Trivett could fail to recognize the woman.

Felicity Dawlish soon came along the gangway, breathless, determined. Then she saw Trivett, and came to a standstill.

Pottle looked at her tense face, and actually felt sorry for her.

Dawlish got out of the taxi outside the house where Louis was, paid the man off, and watched its yellow and black antiquity disappear along a street so narrow that it was surprising that taxis were allowed along it. The engine clattered in the distance.

Dawlish knocked at the door.

It was a plain wooden one, badly in need of a coat of paint. So were the shutters at the windows. That was the one thing which really worried him; none of the shutters was back. It was possible that the others had left, during the night; and he had been sleeping. But there were limits to endurance, and no one would ever know how much sleep he had lost, or the effect of the physical ordeal of the past ten days. Last night he had been at the end of his tether; and he had realized that he might make a fatal blunder if he went on without some sleep.

Now, he waited.

Tim, and probably Mepita, were at the window of the hotel just across the narrow road, watching, waiting. Tim hadn't wanted Dawlish to come; but nothing short of physical violence would have prevented it.

Nothing moved.

Could there be such an anti-climax? Was the house empty? Had he wasted . . .

There were footsteps.

He felt his body go tense.

Then the footsteps stopped, there was a sound at the door and a moment later it opened. He hadn't the faintest idea what to expect, but he saw the last person in the world he would have dreamed of seeing now—the Blonde Doll. There she stood, wearing a bright green linen suit, nice to look at, with a good figure, shapely legs, and a kind of courage. She wasn't really surprised to see him; that meant that he had been seen approaching.

"Hallo, Blondie," Dawlish said brightly, "there aren't many señoritas with the same coloured hair as you. Keeping well?"

She said: "Are you crazy?"

"Great Scott, yes! Didn't you know?" He looked down at her, shaking his head sadly. "I'm beginning to understand all your mistakes, my pet, you must have thought that I was sane and therefore quite predictable. Your bad luck. How's Louis?"

She stood aside.

He went in. He had Mepita's automatic in his hip pocket and the gunman's in his coat; he also had a knife, tied round the calf of his leg; all very melodramatic, as he knew well, but in an emergency it could be useful.

The hall was narrow and gloomy, there was the usual smell of garlic and olive oil. The street door closed, and the woman was behind him—close behind.

A man came from a room ahead of Dawlish.

He wasn't so tall as Dawlish by two inches. He had the same fresh, tanned complexion and his hair was a shade darker, if anything. He wore no make-up, didn't appear to have used artifice to help him—and in a crowd and in poor light—or to anyone who knew Dawlish only slightly—he would have passed for Dawlish. His eyes weren't the cornflower blue of Dawlish's, but they were blue; a slaty shade.

Neither man moved; neither spoke for a long time. Then Dawlish grinned, as if he had no care in the world.

"Why, brother," he said, "we ought to go into our ancestors' history, oughtn't we?"

The man named Louis didn't relax. Lines at his mouth and eyes betrayed the strain he was living under. That made him even more dangerous, just as Mepita had been dangerous with the gun the previous night.

The woman behind Dawlish might be as desperate.

"Or shall we delve into Sep Lee's history?" asked Dawlish. "Nice little past he has, and quite a present. Not," he added brightly, "to mention the future. You shouldn't have killed Corez, you know. Until then it wasn't a hanging job."

"I shan't hang," Louis said abruptly.

Dawlish chuckled. "The old illusion. I must have heard the same famous last words from twenty people who afterwards dangled over the trap doors. The police, like the Mounties, always get their man."

"They'll get you," Louis rasped.

He wasn't sure of himself, and kept glancing over Dawlish's

shoulder at the woman. She was undoubtedly as confused and bewildered as Louis.

That was odd. Wasn't it?

"You wait and see," said Dawlish, comfortably. "You'll find out that even bright boys can make grievous mistakes. I have a little Spanish lass, a lady called Mepita. And when she tells her story, Lew, you'll really want to beat her. Aren't I in scanning form this morning? Or is that rhyming?" He took out cigarettes, lit one, then slid the case back into his pocket. He puffed smoke over Louis's head. "Do I make myself clear?"

Louis said: "You haven't a chance in hell."

He spoke without confidence; in its way, this was a revelation. This man had not planned these crimes. Someone with a needle-sharp mind, astute, swift-thinking, brilliantly clever in certain ways, had done that. But here was the man who had made the mistakes, such as sending O'Flynn to Fernandez's hotel; and marrying Mepita. The astounding, the bewildering thing was that Mepita should have been fooled by him. Apart from his looks, and they weren't exactly the looks of an Adonis, he seemed to have little to offer.

"So I haven't a chance," said Dawlish, and chuckled, as if he were really amused. "We'll see. Where's Carlos?"

"Forget Carlos," Louis growled. "I want—"

He stopped.

There was a sharp tap at the door, and Dawlish knew then that he had been expecting another caller, had been playing for time. Dawlish turned his head, and flattened himself against the wall. But no one he recognized was there when the girl opened the door. Instead, a small, dark-haired man, with one eye discoloured and obviously sightless, the other glowing and quite beautiful, stepped into the hall. The Blonde Doll closed the door behind him.

"Well?" Louis barked.

The little man stared at Dawlish.

"No one has come with him," he said in good English very carefully enunciated. "I was outside when he come. I find the taxi-driver, and he pick up this man in the big square. Then, he was alone. When he comes here, he was alone. So—no one is with him."

"That's all I wanted to know," Louis said, and he seemed to grow in stature, because his confidence came surging back. "You damned fool, Dawlish, did you think—"

"Don't *you* ever think?" asked Dawlish. "Don't you realize that—"

He heard the little newcomer move, saw the upraised hand, and felt a blow on his temple.

It was as if death had called and swallowed him up.

CHAPTER XXI

ONE ALIVE

It was not death.

Dawlish came round in a dimly lit room; and knew at once that the light was the light of day. He did not move for a long time. He began to remember everything—and he was surprised to find himself alive.

He was lying on his back.

His head ached, and he felt nausea in the pit of his stomach.

He could see something close to him, a golden kind of blur. He couldn't make it out. It was as if someone had splashed gold paint about. As his head and his vision cleared he knew that it wasn't paint, but hair. Blonde hair. Blonde Doll. What was *she* doing here?

He licked his lips.

"Blondie!" he called, but the word was only a croak and she couldn't hear it. She had nice hair. He shifted his position a little, so that he could see her face. It wasn't a bad face, either. He could see one cheek and the tip of her nose and her lashes.

He caught his breath.

"Blondie!" he cried.

She didn't move. The fear came upon him that she would never move again, because she was dead. He began to get up. His head was like a balloon—a balloon which had been filled with expanding gas.

He got to his feet with an effort which left him gasping. His head seemed to be on fire. He leaned against a wall, gasping for breath. The golden hair went round and round in shimmering waves, but gradually it steadied, the room stood still. Dawlish moved forward, until he could see Blondie from the front.

Her throat was cut.

There was no knife, but there was blood soaking into the polished wood of the floor.

He went forward and made sure that she was dead.

He tried to adjust himself to this, to understand why this had happened, to decide what he should do.

Get out, of course.

He smelt whisky. The smell had been there all the time, but he had only just started to think about it. His clearer vision showed him a bottle, nearly empty, and a glass by the side of a large armchair. Then he sniffed more vigorously, and realized that the whisky smell didn't come from the bottle, but from his shirt. That was damp. He lowered his head and sniffed, and knew then that the front of his shirt was soaked in whisky; as a man's who had been hopelessly drunk might be.

Why?

That was always the question—why? Why had they selected him in the first place? Why kill Blondie?

Here he was, alone with a dead, a murdered woman.

He looked away from the gash in her neck, and put his hand to his pocket, a mechanical movement, for cigarettes. He felt his case, and beneath his coat, something else which was unfamiliar. He put a hand to his belt, and felt a knife—a sheathed one sticking through the belt and resting against his thigh. He drew it out. He took the blade out of the sheath, and saw drying blood, with bright red streaks where it had scraped against the sheath while being drawn out.

He went to a wash basin, and washed the knife, then left it in hot water, to soak out blood from joints and crevices.

Then he looked at the dead Blonde Doll again.

"I see," he said thickly. "I see."

He began to comprehend other things. His prints would be in this room, on that bottle and the glass, everywhere; he wouldn't have a chance of getting rid of them. Sooner or later the body would be found and the police would come, and then the hunt would be on in earnest. He didn't realize that it had already started and was near.

He dried the knife, put it into his belt, then moved towards the patch of daylight and, going, took more notice of the room. It was long and narrow. The windows were open, but the latticed shutters outside were closed; letting in only slanting light. He peered through and saw the fountain playing, and people walking to and fro purposefully, a donkey cart trundling along, two policemen in bright uniform, a car—and *Trivett*.

Trivett himself was coming here.

There was Trivett, sitting beside the driver of the car which was nosing its way along the narrow street, and being held up by the donkey cart which carried one huge wine barrel.

The police drew nearer.

Dawlish moved very swiftly, reached the door and turned the handle—but the door wouldn't budge. Of course, they would lock him in, make sure that he couldn't get out. Would they? Wouldn't that make the police wonder, would a murderer lock himself in? What the hell did it matter now, the door *was* locked? It opened inwards. Had they left him his own knife, with the pick-lock?

He snatched at his pocket, and the knife was there.

His hand trembled.

"Look, Dawlish," he said aloud, "you have to get out of here; don't panic."

His hand steadied as metal scraped on metal, but it seemed an age before the lock clicked back. There were other sounds in the house. Had the police arrived? Were they forcing their way in, or were they already coming up the stairs?

Where was Trivett?

The lock clicked. Dawlish pulled the door open and stepped into a narrow passage. There was some light from a small window. He heard footsteps on the stairs, leisurely and deliberate. The passage turned, near the window, and he reached the corner and for a moment, at least, was out of sight.

A flight of wooden steps faced him, to a loft or attic. He went up, making more noise than he wanted to on the wooden rungs.

He heard a whistle, followed by a barked command from outside.

He reached the top floor. It was a low room, with sloping ceilings and with a long window. He went to this, crouching; there was no room to stand upright. He looked out, and saw the police in the narrow street, the car waiting, Trivett and a Spanish official getting out; all very formal. A crowd had gathered and was getting thicker—a crowd of people; some well dressed and some in tatters, blind and halt and maim, old men and old women and tiny children, a woman with a child at her breast, donkeys heavily laden with unfamiliar burdens and another with a huge barrel, all looking at the police, and at the door below.

Dawlish looked away from them.

The roof of the house across the narrow street was very near; six feet at most. Could he cross that gap?

If he couldn't there was no hope of escape.

He had not yet reached the stage of thinking beyond the moment, although a nagging worry was already in his mind: about Tim and Mepita. Were they all right?

He leaned out of the window, and stretched one great arm up, clutching the side of the roof. Something jutted out there, and he was able to get a firm grip. He looked down again. Those hundreds of olive faces and hundreds of pairs of bright, dark eyes were all turned towards the door. Two policemen were thundering on it, a pointless business, but a formality which gave him time. A balcony jutting out at the floor below gave him a little cover.

He edged himself further out of the window.

It was agonizing—but at last he could reach the roof with both hands, and haul himself up; but from that moment he could not look down and see whether he was observed.

The balcony gave good cover here.

He hauled himself up, slowly. His feet scraped on the window-ledge and made more noise than he wanted. The banging on the door ceased. There was the murmur of a crowd, and the ring of voices, and Trivett's clear English voice.

Now Dawlish hung from the roof, feet level with the window. He hauled himself up by his great arms until he reached the roof. Then he hauled himself over, and no one shouted, no one appeared to see him. He lay flat on the flat roof, gasping for breath. Now that the supreme effort was over, all the pain came back, his head felt as if it were going to burst and spill the noxious gases upon the crowd.

It steadied.

Dawlish got to his knees, then to his feet, but still crouched low to make sure that he couldn't be seen. Not far along, the roofs of houses on either side of the street were no more than two yards apart. He got slowly towards this place, his feet scraping.

He reached the spot, and for the first time, looked back. The crowd and the car were still there, but Trivett and the official and most of the policemen had gone. They would soon be after him.

Was the other roof sound enough for him to jump? Would it take his weight?

A long skylight gave him no room to take a running jump; it had to be a standing one. He had complete control of his muscles and his nerves now, measured the distance and judged the spot where he wanted to land, drew a deep breath—and leapt.

He landed with a crash, and went sprawling.

He lay still, gasping, knees badly grazed, one arm painful, but he was over. He knew that the crowd must have heard the noise even if they hadn't seen the leaping figure. He got to his knees slowly, crawled back to the edge, and looked down. A few were glancing up and down the street but no one appeared to have associated the noise with the roof.

He crawled along the roof again. Green shutters helped him to locate the hotel where Tim and Mepita should be. It went right through the block, with windows on either street.

Then he had the first big stroke of luck—a fire-escape which led right down to road level. He reached it, and went down with his back to the street. No doubt he would be seen but he didn't hurry, did nothing to arouse an alarm. The solid breadth of the hotel hid him from the police and Trivett, the dead Blonde Doll and Nemesis.

The main entrance to the hotel was in this street. He went in. A different porter was counting out a fistful of dirty-looking peseta notes to a little dark-haired, black-eyed man who glanced at Dawlish curiously, and then looked away. Dawlish did not speak, but went to the stairs and up, and along the passage towards his room. Tim and Mepita must have noticed the crowd. Surely Tim would have tried to distract attention, to help him.

Or had Tim met trouble?

Nonsense thoughts.

He reached the bedroom, and turned the handle, thrust open the door, and went in.

Louis, who could look so startlingly like him, faced him with a gun and a grin. The door of the smaller room, behind him, was closed.

There he was, grinning, showing good teeth, with back to the window and the daylight. Outside were the noises of the crowd and the impatient cries of people who wanted to get by. Trivett and the Spanish police were searching the house now that they had discovered the murdered woman.

"Shut the door," Louis said, "and stand still."

Dawlish closed the door.

"So you aren't so clever," Louis sneered. "I saw you on the roof, and it gave me a shock, but—you came from one trap into another."

Dawlish didn't speak; was past even thought.

"It's true we had a bit of luck," Louis said. "One of our helpers noticed Mepita come in, and there's only one senorita like Mepita in this world, isn't there?"

Dawlish just looked.

"What's the matter, lost your tongue?" Louis grinned and sneered. "They told me that nothing really kept you quiet, Dawlish, but they must have made a mistake. How did you get on with Blondie?"

Dawlish moistened his lips with the tip of his tongue.

"The trouble with Blondie was that she got restless," said Louis, "and she didn't like the idea of me marrying Mepita. Imagine! As a matter of fact, it was Mepita or Blondie, and I preferred Mepita every time. She'll be all right. She'll do what she's told because she'll be scared of what might happen to her precious brother if she doesn't." He actually chuckled. "The things poor Mepita doesn't know! But when you've been caught and hanged, if you don't break your neck trying to escape, everything will be all right, won't it? The police will have their crook, I'll be in the clear, and we'll stay wedded. Mepita won't mind a change of name. It's working out my way, and very nicely."

Dawlish said: "So it's working out your way." He saw a box of cigarettes on the bedside table, just out of reach; English cigarettes which Tim must have left there. A book of matches was by its side. He moved across; and Louis raised the gun sharply. Dawlish dropped on to the side of a bed, took a cigarette out, and lit it.

"You might be able to fool Mepita and Carlos but you can't fool everyone all the time," he went on. "Who's your brain, Louis?"

Louis rasped: "What the hell are you talking about?"

"Just the obvious things. Who's your brain? You haven't worked this out at all. You've done what you've been told, but haven't the wit to think two moves ahead." He saw the other flush, and was quite sure that he was right. He had been sure of that for a long time, but how did it help?

Louis wasn't in this on his own. Who had given the orders, worked the whole thing out?

The Blonde Doll?

"You think you're smart," sneered Louis. "Okay, there are

more of us." He grinned and leered again. "Feel any better because of that?"

Dawlish didn't speak.

"So you don't," said Louis. He moved slowly, covering Dawlish all the time; and Dawlish was too far away from him to hope to get at him before he could shoot. "I didn't think you would. Which roof do you want to jump off, Dawlish? Or would you rather be caught and stand trial? Wouldn't be so nice for your wife that way, would it? Did anyone tell you she's in Barcelona?"

The word was wrung from Dawlish. "*No!*"

"Take it from me, she is!" Louis almost gloated over Dawlish's distress. "She reached the airport with Trivett, but my spies tell me that they didn't leave the airport together, perhaps she isn't friends with him any longer. You won't see her again and she won't see you, except as a corpse. Make up your mind—want to jump off a roof and kill yourself to escape trial? Don't say you'd rather stand trial. *I* don't mind—much."

He stopped.

Dawlish finished the cigarette, and stubbed it out, and wondered what would happen when he leapt at the man. Would the bullet strike a vital spot?

Sooner or later he would have to throw himself forward, and put his faith in the gods. He had no choice. But there might be a way of lessening the risk. He kept looking at Louis but could see the other bed—he was between the two. He could drop on all fours then heave this bed up and crash it down on to Louis; that would give him some kind of chance.

The trouble would be with the timing; he must choose a moment when Louis was sure all danger had past.

Then the door of the dressing-room opened wide.

"Always you are the fool," said Carlos Fernandez to Louis,

but his eyes were gay and there was laughter in him. "It is much better that Dawlish does not stand trial. He would talk too much, you should not have locked him in with Blondie. But we do not mind which roof he chooses to jump from, do we?"

CHAPTER XXII

CARLOS

Dawlish stared into the bright, smiling face. Except for his expression, Carlos looked remarkably like his sister; no one could mistake the family likeness. He was young and very handsome, and the gaiety in his eyes would have been a thing to rejoice about had there been a different cause.

"Good morning, Mr. Dawlish," he said.

Dawlish didn't speak.

"He's not talkative," Louis growled.

"I suppose we can't really be surprised about that," said Carlos, brightly. He moved towards the window, and looked out. "Ah, more police are going in."

"Push him out of this window!" Louis said viciously.

"Oh, my poor Louis—it is a good thing I changed sides," Carlos said. "You are not very clever. That would bring the police here, wouldn't it?" His English was better; more colloquial, too.

"I don't care what roof he falls off," Louis said. "Let's fix him."

Outside, only yards away, were the police who would know all they needed to know if they heard only a few sentences from these men; but they might be a million miles away for all the use they were to Dawlish. Supposing he shouted, roared to them, put up a fight? There was Louis's gun; and now one appeared in Carlos's hand. He felt sick at the realization that Carlos was working on the other side. Something had made him switch— perhaps the hope of saving himself from disgrace if he had a share in the loot?

Was he the mind behind all this?

No—he had been in deadly earnest in London. That was beyond all doubt.

Louis said: "Any trouble in there?"

"The man Jeremy is still unconscious," Carlos said. "So is Mepita." So Tim was alive, there was some hope. "It's easy to know what to do with him, he is going to be drowned while bathing!" He chuckled. "But Dawlish wouldn't go for a swim in circumstances like these, would he?"

Louis said: "He won't do anything again, but what are we waiting for?"

There was a pause; a long pause; and then Carlos said:

"We're waiting for Dawlish's wife."

He meant it.

They were expecting Felicity.

There was nothing Dawlish could do but wait.

Nothing had gone right in this affair from the beginning, every chance he had taken had gone sour; and now they were waiting for Felicity.

He felt a physical weakness, a weariness which he could not throw off. He lit another cigarette, and tried to fight against that awful lassitude—a kind of hopelessness which had worsened with the news that Felicity was on her way.

Why had she come?

Why did they want her?

"She won't be long," Carlos Fernandez said, offhandedly. "We had to help her to shake off the police, but that was easy. She will soon be here, and we can finish them both together."

Louis stood up.

"Look," he said, "I don't get it. Why hurt her? Where does she come in?"

Carlos said lightly: "She is a very persistent woman, and she made a little discovery which would have saved Dawlish a lot of trouble if he'd made it first. She knows *him*."

Dawlish sat very still, tense; ready.

"So *that's* it," Louis said, as if he fully understood. "How long will she be?"

"Not long," Carlos said, "don't get impatient. It's all ready now. He's in Barcelona, of course, and he's bringing her along. Mepita will keep quiet, for your sake and for mine—poor Mepita, she doesn't know how wicked her brother has become! With Dawlish and his wife and Jeremy dead, as well as Blondie, we haven't anything to worry about. The only other man who could give anything away is Sep Lee, and he won't—he'll spend a few years in jail, but there'll be a fortune waiting for him when he comes out. There'll be a fortune waiting for everyone— except *poor* Mr. Dawlish." Carlos laughed again. "I don't like the look in his eyes, do you, Louis? I have a distinct impression that in a moment he will try to do violence. That would never do! That—"

Dawlish dropped to the floor.

He saw the change of expression in the Spaniard's face as he fell. He knew that both would shoot. He got his hands beneath the bed which stood between him and the two men, and heaved. The bed rose up on one side. He heard the hiss of a shot from an airgun, then a cry as the bed struck Carlos and pushed him down. Dawlish was still on the floor, fearful of Louis. He grabbed a gun and scrambled to his feet. Carlos was pinned to the floor, Louis had also fallen, and was bleeding from a cut in the forehead.

These were the vital seconds.

Dawlish rounded the bed and snatched Louis's gun. He felt as if new life had been poured into him. Louis's face was twisted in agony; the bed had really injured him. Dawlish didn't move it, just turned round. Carlos Fernandez's gun wasn't in sight, so it must be beneath the bed.

Dawlish locked the room door, then went to the dressing-room door and pushed it open.

There was Tim, sitting back in a chair, chin on his chest and dead to the world. There was Mepita, looking very, very beautiful, and looking dazed as if she were waking from a deep sleep.

They stood staring at each other.

"But such a beeg noise, I hear."

Dawlish heard footsteps approaching the room, and hurried to the door. A man called out in Spanish.

"Everything's all right?!" Dawlish called.

"What you say, sir?"

"Everything is all right."

"But such a beeg noise, I hear."

"I knocked over a table."

The man outside gave up, and walked away.

Mepita was wide awake, now.

Tim still slept. Dawlish went to him and made sure that he wasn't badly hurt, and was breathing steadily.

But it wasn't all over yet.

Soon, Felicity would be here, and '*he*'. Dawlish had to wait until then, there was nothing he could do until each had arrived. Yet he was not free from the oppressive sense of danger; urgent, pressing menace. There were others who worked for Louis and Carlos; danger might come from unsuspected quarters. That one, gigantic effort had given him a chance, but he had to hold the chance.

"It is—the real Pat-rick," Mepita said.

"That's right," said Dawlish. He moved across to Tim, and felt his pulse; it was all right, he didn't think there was much the matter with Tim. He turned to Mepita, as she began to say:

"But you—you were a prisoner."

"That's right," agreed Dawlish. "All ready for the hanging or the fall off a roof." He fought back a desire to shout at her. "If you see what I mean. And you were to hold your tongue, Mepita. You were to live with your murdering husband and murdering brother. I wonder if you would have done." He wiped the sweat from his forehead, and wondered why he was talking like this; it was as if words had been dammed up inside him and had broken loose now; and he could do nothing to check the torrential flow. "Not so good for you, was it, lovely Mepita? Would you have lived a lie, I wonder?"

Her eyes were the most beautiful eyes he had ever seen, the colour of chestnuts fresh from their green husk. Her hair was so lovely, too, and here was beauty such as few men would ever see. What was in her mind? Was she goodness itself, as everyone who knew a little of her seemed to think? Or did she harbour evil?

"Where is—Carlos?" she asked.

"He slipped and hurt himself."

"And—Louis?"

"I don't think Louis is feeling too good," said Dawlish. "In fact—"

"Pat-rick," Mepita said, and drew closer to him; and she was so beautiful, a thing he could not forget. And she was deter-mined that he should not forget it. He knew that, now. Beauty and goodness might live together in her, but she was a woman first. "Pat-rick," she said, "if the police find Louis they—they will believe it is *you*."

He didn't speak.

"Is that not true?" she demanded.

He said: "They might do, yes."

She didn't know that Trivett would never make a mistake about his identity, but that wasn't the thing that mattered. Show Trivett someone who could be Dawlish's double, and Trivett would reason the rest out. Mepita had been quick to see the possibilities; she had a mind.

"But do not be absurd, of course that is what the police would think," said Mepita. "You would be free, Pat-trick. There would be no danger."

"That's right," said Dawlish.

"Then kill him," she said softly, "*kill* him. He will not harm Carlos more, then. We can get our jewels back. Perhaps—perhaps you and I . . ." she was much nearer, so near that her hands were touching his and she was trying to draw him close to her. And her eyes were so luminous, so lovely. He could feel the passion in her, too, something he had never sensed before, but she was trying to make a fool of him now; for the sake of her dear brother!

"We can get away, there will be no danger for you, no danger at all."

"So there wouldn't," Dawlish said.

He could thrust her savagely away from him, and tell her what he thought; thrust proffered beauty away. Or he could let her think that he would play the game the way she wanted it. He didn't waste time thinking of the miserable truth; of the cold-ness of her heart and of her callousness. Let the man she had married die, she said, let them go away together, let them save themselves and Carlos above all.

He could have struck her.

Instead, he gripped her arms so tightly that it hurt, but she did not cry out or protest or try to free herself, there was something almost animal in the way she gloried in his great strength.

"Let's kill him," she said, "and go. We . . ." she stopped and moved towards the door. For the first time she saw the upturned bed, and Carlos, and Louis, with the wound in his forehead. She went to Carlos and knelt down, black skirt flaring, her grace of movements so beautiful that it was hard to believe what she had just said and had conceived with a swiftness which proved her capacity for evil.

She stood up.

"There is a back door. Can you carry him?"

"Yes, but—"

"Then hurry," she urged. "We can get a car, I will telephone a friend who will send a large one. Hurry, Patrick!" Her eyes were glowing, her cheeks were flushed, this new excitement gave her a thrill which made her seem younger, lovelier—as if anyone could be lovelier than Mepita Fernandez, who had no heart.

"We can't—" Dawlish began.

"We must hurry! Look!" She spun round, skirt flaring again, blouse pressing tightly against her breast as she moved towards the bedside table. There were the matches. She snatched them up, struck one, held it downwards until the flame touched her finger, and then held it against a sheet. It began to smoulder, blacken and to flame. "Look! We can burn the room, they will think he died that way. *Look!*" She dropped the match and left it to burn, with the smoke rising up from the sheet, the smell pungent and frightening. She picked up a pillow and thrust it into Dawlish's hands. "Use that, smother him, they will think—"

He put out a great foot and stamped the fire out. She was startled, and scowled at him, with the pillow still in her hands.

"Why do you do that?"

"You've a lot to learn in the ways of bad men," Dawlish said, and took the pillow away, tossed it across the room, and gave her a bear hug which almost forced the wind out of her body. "Dumb brunette," he said, inanely. "There's still someone who could give us away."

"*Is* there?" That startled her, she stared wide-eyed.

"You ought to know." That she seemed surprised was puzzling. "There's the Boss. Haven't you heard them talking about him?"

"Is *he* coming?" she asked, and looked astonished. "Oh, yes, I have heard about him, often they have talked of a man who sends their orders, but—will *you* take another man's orders?"

"Not for long," said Dawlish. "Just long enough to serve our purpose, my Mepita. First I want to see who he is, then I have to know what he proposes to do. It might be as well to burn him, too."

He laughed.

She also laughed as if it were a great joke, and a thrill to anticipate.

"Don't you know him?"

"Not yet."

"Are you sure he is coming?"

"He told Carlos so."

"Oh, yes, there was some talk of it," said Mepita. "I will not allow Carlos to be hurt more, you understand. He was foolish to get into debt, but he is not bad."

She really believed that it was so simple; kill Louis, get safely away, have nothing more to fear. No wonder she had been so gullible before. She followed her own whims, was a creature of her own swift changing emotions.

There was no point in arguing with her, yet.

"Mepita . . ." Dawlish began.

"Yes?"

"When I came into your room last night, did you know Carlos was working with Louis?"

"I was afraid so," she said, "but it is because he is so frightened. I can understand poor Carlos."

Dawlish had a strange impression that she was trying to tell him the truth as she saw it.

"All our lives we have been poor," she went on. "Oh, we have had some money, and the apartment is paid for by a good uncle, but always we are so very poor. Is it wicked to be rich?" She slipped into the graphic present tense again. "First Carlos talks of selling these jewels and persuades me that it would be a good thing. Then I fall in love with Louis. He is bad, I do not know, Carlos does not know. Suddenly Carlos discovers he is bad, that he will perhaps not sell the jewels and give us the money. So— Carlos is desperate, is he not? Are we to blame him if, to save the money, to keep free from trouble, he decides to work with these others?"

She seemed to long for Dawlish to say no.

Then the telephone bell rang.

CHAPTER XXIII

THE BOSS

Dawlish turned sharply away from Mepita, and looked at the black instrument. It had suddenly become a thing of menace.

The bell rang again.

Dawlish said thinly: "Answer it, Mepita. Tell them that Louis made you do so."

"Yes," she said, at once, and moved towards the instrument. The strange, almost the unbelievable thing was that she could be so naïve. She was herself; whatever she decided to do there was that fascinating naturalness about her. 'Bad' and 'evil' were not the proper words.

She lifted the telephone and spoke quickly; then paused.

Then she spoke again, and put the receiver down.

"The boss comes," she said. "That was Pedro, who works for Louis, to say that he is coming now. Also—a woman is with him. Did you know about that woman?"

Dawlish said very softly: "No, Mepita, I didn't know." He had to lie, because he was not sure how she would react if he told her the truth. There was no need to risk that now.

"What will you do?" Mepita asked.

"Wait until he comes," said Dawlish. "Don't worry." He took the gun out of his pocket. "You sit there," he said, and pointed to a chair which was almost opposite the door. "He will be surprised when he sees you, and I'll be able to deal with him."

She said: "It is a clever idea!" and went and sat down.

Dawlish unlocked the passage door, stood by the dressing-room. Whoever came in would see Mepita first, then that end of the room which was not chaotic. Not until they came right in would they see the two unconscious men, the upturned bed and the evidence of the fight.

Footsteps sounded.

Here was the man—and Felicity.

Dawlish's heart pounded. He kept his gun inside his pocket, with his fingers about it. Mepita sat very primly, knees close together, demure and lovely; she was already setting her face in the smile which Dawlish knew well. She wanted to save Carlos, that seemed her only concern now.

But was it possible to be certain? Was she only pretending to be so casual about Louis?

The footsteps drew closer.

The handle turned.

The door opened quickly. Felicity was thrust into the room. Behind her came a man who entered swiftly, caught sight of Mepita and stopped, agape.

It was Maurice Gale, senior partner in *Gale's*.

It was a tableau.

Felicity, two yards in front of Gale, stared first at Mepita and then at Dawlish. And Gale, rigid, one hand at a coat pocket, the other held in front of his chest. He didn't see Dawlish in those first few seconds, had eyes only for Mepita, and her smile, her beauty, were enough to hypnotize any man. Gale was shocked at sight of her, hadn't expected her to be here.

Then Dawlish said: "Hallo, my darling. Move aside, will you?"

He had his gun out, now, covering Gale. "Hallo, Maurice, what a surprise!"

Maurice Gale turned, but did not utter a word, just looked dumbfounded.

Now Dawlish knew just what had happened; understood everything that mattered. Here was Gale, who owned the shop, who had probably been trading in stolen jewels and *objets d'art* for years, who had got away when he thought the moment ripe, and then started the campaign to have Dawlish framed for everything that was wrong at *Gale's.* If he had succeeded, and he had come very near, then he could have gone back and carried on with the business, his name and reputation as good as ever they had been. All his talk of wanting to travel for the business, needing a locum in London, of being able to trust both Pat and Felicity Dawlish, had been dust in the Dawlishes' eyes.

Nothing else needed explaining now.

Sep Lee had worked for Gale, of course; and lied for him. The man named Louis had been found because a man like Dawlish was essential to the plot—a pretty plot, a clever and brilliant plot, and worse because it had been planned and carried out by a friend.

Felicity said in a gasping voice: "Oh, Pat!"

"It isn't good now, Maurice, is it?" Dawlish said, and his voice was very hard. "And it looked as if it was going to work out so nicely. Did you guess, Fel?"

"Yes," she said, in a husky voice. "At least, I began to wonder. It all began when he'd gone away, but Sep Lee seemed a connecting link with something that had happened before. And I saw a picture of that woman, the Blonde Doll. She's like Maurice, isn't she?"

Like *Maurice*.

And Tim had said: 'I've seen her before, somewhere.'

"He's told me, now," said Felicity. "She's his half-sister." Felicity paused. "Pat, what—what are we going to do?"

Then, before Dawlish could answer and while Maurice Gale stood silent, as if shocked beyond all words by this, Mepita spoke. She stood up, very slowly. Her eyes sparkled, as if the fire had been freshly kindled. In all the magnificence of her beauty, she moved towards Dawlish and put a hand on his arm.

She said: "Who is this man?"

"He's the master mind, Mepita," Dawlish told her very softly. "He's plotted everything. He's turned Carlos bad. He's the man who put Louis up to all his tricks, deceived you, and tricked and cheated Carlos."

He spoke with bitterness that made him forget Mepita's hatred for the man behind all this. She moved swiftly, banging against his gun arm. Maurice Gale snatched a gun from his pocket and pushed Felicity aside.

He fired.

Dawlish felt the wind of the bullet.

Dawlish thrust Mepita away; she caught her leg against a chair and fell backwards. Dawlish leapt forward, as Gale tried to level his gun again, but Felicity stopped him, striking the hand which held it.

Then Dawlish reached Maurice Gale.

There was the man's handsome face and terrified eyes. It receded. It seemed to be lost, as if in a great, oozy mist. Dawlish clutched the throat and his great fingers buried themselves in the flesh. He squeezed. All the savagery that could be in man was in him then because of the great denial of trust, because of a sudden cataclysmic surge of hatred for the man who had planned this thing for so long and with such cunning. He *wanted* to kill.

He heard Felicity's voice and felt something tugging at his arm, but he ignored it. Then he felt blows at his cheek, but none was strong enough to weaken his grip on the other's throat. The mist in front of his eyes was tinged with red. He knew what he was doing, and yet he was not quite himself; it was as if there were two men in him, the killer and the man he knew.

Then he felt a gust of wind; stronger hands clutched him; a blow caught him on the side of the face, and he staggered. Something sharp struck his wrists, and he winced and snatched his hands away. The mist began to clear. He saw other men, and Maurice Gale on the floor, with one man on his knees beside him. He saw Felicity. He saw Trivett. He saw the blood at his own wrists, where someone had slashed him with a knife to make him let go. Felicity moved forward, but Trivett stopped her and grabbed a pillow, stripped the case from it and began to dab the blood.

Dawlish swallowed hard.

"Tim," he said. "In there. Other room."

"All right," said Trivett. His voice seemed to come from a long way off. "All over. Here you are, Fel."

Felicity took the pillow-case. The cuts were only superficial and they did not really hurt. Maurice Gale was stretched out on the floor, with a Spaniard bending over him, giving artificial respiration. Others were bending over Louis and Carlos. By the dressing-room, a Spanish official, speaking good English, was telling Trivett to handle the Inglisi as he wished. Trivett thanked him warmly, then came back to Dawlish:

"Tim's sleeping the sleep of the unjust," he said.

"Feeling—funny?" croaked Dawlish. He wanted to sit down,

and Felicity realized it and led him to the bed; he dropped on to it. "Because—I'm not. You see—what happened."

"Oh, yes," said Trivett. He spoke quite calmly, showed no excitement; but he was hot, sweat was running down his face. "Fel and I had a chat, coming over. She said that she was coming to see Maurice Gale, that he'd told her that he could help. And she'd already told me about the likeness between the Blonde Doll and Gale. So we arranged for Fel to come ahead with Gale—but they were followed. For once," Trivett went on, and forced a wry smile, "you can hand it to the Yard."

Dawlish closed his eyes.

"The Yard can have it," he said. "All of it, from this day on." He opened his eyes. "There's a woman in here who looks like an angel and has the philosophy of a pagan," he said. "All she cares about is her Carlos."

"Poor Mepita," Felicity said.

Mepita was by her brother now; fearful for him. Her lovely hair, burnished by the sun, spread over her head like a canopy, and she could not see her face. She then saw Louis, able to walk, and Carlos with a broken leg, being taken off.

The narrow street was thronged with eager, curious people; donkey carts; small children; and the brilliant sun.

CHAPTER XXIV

SHOP FOR SALE

The sun shone brightly, and the Mediterranean, blue as its fame, rippled away into the distance. Dawlish and Felicity and Tim Jeremy sat on pale sand beneath the shade of a huge umbrella and watched the dancing light upon the water and nearer at hand, children playing, and two or three señoritas, each quite beautiful, heedless of the law and lying on their backs so that the sun could tan their skin to an even darker hue.

Each reminded Dawlish of Mepita.

Many things reminded Dawlish of Mepita. She had not been held, but Carlos had, and she seemed lost and near despair. But the uncle who paid for the rent of the apartment was looking after her; and would try to help Carlos escape some of the consequences of his folly.

Trivett was tidying up odds and ends and accepting the eager hospitality of the Spanish police. He was due here, soon, at the little spot of the Costa Brava which Tim had selected, and Felicity had insisted they should visit. For, she said, Dawlish might not realize it, but he was almost dead on his feet.

They knew, now, how Tim had been fooled by a maid at the

hotel, bribed to help Gale's men, been knocked out, robbed of his gun, and drugged. He was better now, although sore in spirit.

They had lazed and rested, talked, and idled away the time, waiting for Trivett—who would come and tell them when he won his battle with the Spanish authorities for Dawlish. He had been hopeful when he had last seen Dawlish, that the story of the death of Webber and of the Blonde Doll would be accepted. Much depended on a Spanish crook's evidence.

On the road close to the beach, between them and the white and pink and yellow houses, the waving palms, the orange trees, the camellias growing carelessly on bushes and huge patches of bougainvillæa, there came a car. Dawlish turned to look at it. He wore shorts and a silk shirt and a loose scarf. Felicity, in a flowered dress with a floppy hat, looked round too.

"Here he is," she announced.

"The great Superintendent Trivett," said Tim Jeremy, in a sonorous voice. "Poor old boy. Look at him—dressed for the English winter!"

Trivett came briskly from the car, spruce in navy blue which it was almost hot to look at. He had left his trilby behind. In his few days here he had made friends with the sun and his skin was looking three shades darker than when he had arrived. The anxiety which had shown for days before Dawlish had left England had gone completely; he looked clear-eyed, satisfied, a man who had accomplished his purpose.

The men stood up, and waved to chairs, and a waiter hovered and was sent off for long drinks and ice.

"Hallo, Fel," said Trivett. "How are the savages behaving?"

"Indolently," answered Felicity.

"Catching mood," said Tim. "I got mine from the police." Trivett grinned.

"You don't improve much," he declared. "Well, Pat, it's all over bar the shouting. I've got everything fixed, and you can go as soon as the inquest is over."

"What, no stain?" asked Tim.

"No stain on your characters," said Trivett prosily. "I've been in constant touch with the Yard, of course, and Sep Lee's broken down there, too. Now we've all the corroboration that we ever wanted. The plot was simple, Pat. Gale was in a bad jam for money. He and Sep Lee started the fencing, to get out of it. Then they wanted to cut loose and live honest lives, but too many people knew that the business was involved in fencing. So they thought up the nice one to involve you. Sep did some colourful lying, through contact men, so that everyone who knew that *Gale's* were buying hot stuff believed that you had a financial interest all the time, and that neither Lee nor Maurice Gale were involved. Lee measured the risks carefully; he knew he'd get a long sentence, but he'd salted a small fortune away.

"Gale was the brains behind it, of course. He'd even fixed up your double, Louis, and had Louis Barnett study you, at a distance, in several places in Europe, so as to be able to impersonate you. Maurice Gale also used his half-sister, and she was getting along nicely with Louis Barnett until the Spanish business cropped up."

Dawlish said lazily: "How did it?"

"Exactly the way you were told. Spain was a good country to sell to, with a lot of rich men with money to spare, as well as a lot of visitors from abroad, especially from the United States, all ready for bargains. Barnett and Gale established a small agency over here, but wanted someone to sell to the aristocracy, as it were. Carlos de Ciento y Fernandez had a good name, came of a good family, and was ideal—and he'd got himself in trouble. They planned to blackmail him into helping, but things misfired when he introduced his sister to the Spanish agent, and in his absence the agent introduced her to Louis. Louis had been built up in her eyes as a wealthy Englishman—the story that her brother had told her, to keep her quiet. Louis had a way with him, and—well, he married her, intending, he swears, to regularize the marriage as soon as he could.

"The bond between him and the Blonde Doll was never very tight," said Trivett. "The thing which Louis and Gale didn't expect was the London visit. No one could ever predict what Mepita was going to do. Don't you agree, Tim? Or shall I use simpler words?"

"Eh?" grunted Tim. "Oh, *words*. I thought you were making animal noises. Don't mind me."

"I'm following," Felicity said. "Just."

Trivett grinned.

"I don't know how you do it," he said. "Always so strictly honest and married to—but never mind. Bear in mind that Mepita really believed that she was married to our Patrick Dawlish. Corez, a friend of the family and in love with Mepita, believed that Louis was up to no good. He'd been in England some time, checking. He got hold of that photograph, taken on a day when you were somewhere else, Pat—proof that there was funny business. With the proof, he wanted to break up the whole gang, but Louis got wind of it, and had Corez attacked, and later murdered. The photograph was missing, though—Corez had it—and O'Flynn was sent to see if you had it.

"Remember that behind it all was the plan to leave you holding the baby, Pat," Trivett went on. "Then Maurice Gale would hear what had happened, and using an alias and a false passport, came to England to handle the situation. Sep Lee was to be dead by then. Certainly Gale did his damnedest. He believed that if the police really thought you had lost your head, were guilty and trying to cover up, it would keep them from worrying too much about any other angle, such as Mepita and Carlos. So he started the hare, whisked brother and sister away—and then Allison snarled things a bit."

Trivett paused, to drink ice cold orange squash.

"Bill," said Felicity sweetly, "Pat did put Allison on to the case, you know. I've been thinking of something you said at that hotel in the Casco Antiguo—that this was a police success. I'm not at all sure you're right. In fact I'm not sure. If you'd had your way, Pat would have been arrested weeks ago. If you'd caught him in Soho that night he would have been put on trial—admit it!"

Dawlish smiled faintly at her vehemence.

Trivett said defensively: "Well, there was a lot of evidence, Fel. The Soho business. That was laid on by Gale, by the way, using two or three old lags who played a part. It was neatly planned, like the rest of it. Lee was to have been killed but didn't know it—he thought the bullet which got him was an accident. In any case, he'd a fortune salted away—no one else could touch it. He wanted to be sentenced and get it over, of course. I agree that Pat would probably have had to stand trial, but a good counsel could have torn a lot of the case to bits."

"After all," muttered Tim, "why not? Only a police case."

"What about the Kroo emeralds?" Dawlish asked.

"We had the tip—and Sep Lee didn't know we were going to raid *Gale's* when we did. He didn't get them away in time."

"Nice work by Scotland Yard," Dawlish grinned.

"You can forgive too much," Felicity declared. "If it were me, I'd remind Bill for ever and a day that he and the Yard made an awful hash."

"All right, I'll come between the pair of you," Dawlish said peaceably.

"There isn't a great deal more to talk about," Trivett said. "It's been going on for a long time of course. The Spanish police are quite satisfied that you didn't have anything to do with it. I've had some trouble persuading them that your statement about the way the man died at Mepita's flat was accurate, but Mepita has corroborated. Incidentally, Gale was afraid she would be too vital a witness for the police—hence Webber's attempt to kill her. Anyway, you won't have to stand trial for manslaughter, if they've a manslaughter charge in Spain."

"Thanks," said Dawlish, still lazily.

"Next, please," invited Tim.

"We come to the time when Pat arrived in Barcelona," Trivett said, "and got in touch with you. We now know that you were identified as a friend of Pat's—and as Maurice Gale knew you both, that isn't surprising. So Tim was watched. Everything you did together—and separately, if it comes to that—was known and reported. They wanted to make quite sure that you couldn't get away, and Gale's half-sister was making difficulties about Louis and Mepita. She'd been smoothed over by the assurance that it was only a marriage of convenience, but wasn't too happy. When she saw Mepita, she knew that she certainly couldn't trust Louis. She threatened to talk to the police if he didn't do what she wanted, and—" Trivett shrugged—"they'd become killer-minded. Have you and the blonde in a room together, make it look as if you'd lost your head, killed your partner and then drunk yourself into forgetfulness. They locked you in—a duplicate key was in your pocket, did you know?"

Very sadly, Dawlish shook his head.

"You see," said Tim, brightly, "the police *are* better at some things. All over, then?"

"Case closed, apart from formalities," Trivett agreed. "When are you going home, Pat?"

Dawlish said: "Soon. I've an idea that Fel would like a look at Spain while we're here, and I daresay we could fix some pesetas with your police friends. Trust a copper to find his way about! What about you, Tim?"

"*I'm* going home," Tim said.

The Dawlishes spent ten days in Spain and would gladly have stayed longer; but the formalities in London were greater than Trivett had made out.

Once they had flown back to London, Dawlish had to go through the accounts of *Gale's,* check all sales and all the jewellery which had been bought during the past few years. It was quite a job. The ramifications of the buying and selling of stolen goods went far. It became more and more evident that sooner or later the truth would have come out, and that Maurice Gale had been right when he had wanted a stooge.

His wife had known nothing about it; and she still owned a share in *Gale's.*

"So do we," said Felicity, when Dawlish was talking about it a few days after the trial, Louis and Gale had been sentenced to death, and others of the gang—including Charlie Boy—to long terms of imprisonment. They did not yet know what had happened to Carlos. "But I'll gladly give my share of *Gale's* away," Felicity added.

"You be careful," said Dawlish, showing unusual animation. "We can sell the place, if we have a bit of luck. And then I can buy some more orchards and some more pigs, and then we—"

The telephone bell rang.

Dawlish stretched out a hand.

"Pat-rick Dawlish speaking," he said heartily, and wondered if it were Allison, who had promised to ring, or the police, or anyone at all about the case. Allison had the inside story, a scoop which had delighted him. At first Dawlish showed no enthusiasm about this call—but suddenly Felicity saw a change in him. His eyes shone. His mouth opened. He expressed something that was not far removed from fatuous delight.

"Take it from me I don't mind!" he roared into the telephone. "Just name the day . . . Yes . . . Yes . . . YES!" he boomed, and added: "I'll be seeing you, goodbye!" He banged the receiver down and jumped up, grabbed Felicity and hugged her, kissed her and then, in an excess of exuberance, swung her round and round. She clung on to him desperately until he had stopped the crazy pirouetting, and stammered:

"W-w-w-what *is* it?"

"The Gregory couple don't want to stay at the old Homestead," he cried. "Will we release them from their contract and go back to the pigs and the apples and peace in the countryside? Did you hear me say *yes?*"

Felicity put her head on one side.

"Peace," she said, "is one of the things you'll never know anything about. But yes, darling, let's go."

They were back in their house, Four Ways, in the heart of rural Surrey, when a letter arrived with a Spanish postmark. Dawlish opened this and Felicity read with him, over his shoulder.

It was from Mepita.

She was very apologetic, and obviously chastened. Carlos was in prison; if his conduct was good he would be out in a year. The Spanish police had taken a merciful view of the part he had played. Mepita said that she was teaching young people English, she was being very good, she was very, very sorry to have been so much trouble.

"Provided we never see her again, I shall always have a soft spot for Mepita," Felicity said.

ABOUT THE AUTHOR

John Creasey, born in 1908, was a paramount English crime and science fiction writer who used myriad pseudonyms for more than six hundred novels. He founded the UK Crime Writers' Association in 1953. In 1962, his book *Gideon's Fire* received the Edgar Award for Best Novel from the Mystery Writers of America. Many of the characters featured in Creasey's titles became popular, including George Gideon of Scotland Yard, who was the basis for a subsequent television series and film. Creasey died in Salisbury, UK, in 1973.

THE PATRICK DAWLISH MYSTERIES

FROM OPEN ROAD MEDIA

EARLY BIRD BOOKS

FRESH DEALS, DELIVERED DAILY

Love to read?
Love great sales?

Get fantastic deals on bestselling ebooks delivered to your inbox every day!

Sign up today at
earlybirdbooks.com/book